The Trials of Boy Kings

The Trials of Boy Kings

Chosen King Book II

M.J. Sewall

Contents

This book is dedicated to my sister Janet

If it weren't for you...

I begin the tale again
In the middle of our story
The two boy kings
Linked by equal danger
Divided by a large world
New threats and new truths emerge
For some, the story will end
For those that survive
They will be changed forever
This part of the story is filled with fire and blood

~ Llawes the Younger

Also by M J Sewall

Chosen King
  Book 1: Dream of Empty Crowns
  Book 3: Plague of Tyrants

Forever Warriors
Wild Monsters Dance About – Stories From An Unruly Mind
Seven Ways To Jane

Chapter 1

Monsters

The monsters were getting out of hand.

The large watership bobbed in the gray day, as the waters mesmerized the man standing on deck. The cold wind swirled around his muscular frame, and played with his beard. Bare chested, he refused to let the cold touch him.

He willed it away.

"A fin, two hundred feet off deck, father," said one of the crew rushing up to him. The man knew this was the first time the boy had been on a large watership, the youngest son of an important man from the inner council.

The older man patted the young man's face that held only the wisp of a beard. "Let's go kill it."

The young man smiled and yelled to the crew. "Long boats at the ready!"

The man smiled as he saw the crew begin to lower the long boats. *Just like the legends*, he thought. He jumped into one of the three boats as the winches lowered the narrow wooden vessels into the waters.

The man shouted, "Are you ready to reclaim your place in history?" the six men on his boat cheered as the man spoke. "Our ancestors hunted these monsters back in the mists of time. Now they have returned. Let's send them back into legend!"

The crew of young men cheered louder. They treated the man like a god. That worried him. *The old superstitions must die for us to finish our work*, thought the man. *Best to show them that I am a man, and that a man is more than any god ever could be.*

He couldn't tell his crew that he had other reasons for killing these beasts. Three of his airships had gone missing. That was not a coincidence. All of them had been lost over the waters, no survivors. I will not let these things take my ships one by one, he thought. *It's time to fight.*

He had trained the young men himself. Getting this close to a dangerous monster in the open waters required teamwork. He had grilled the men for weeks before they made this journey. Rowing, rowing, and rowing again in unison until they could not lift their arms. To train men to think as one, to have one goal, you had to break down their bodies first. *Isn't that what Ollander used to say?* The man shook off the rhythmic rowing that made his thoughts wander to his old friend. The friend he was forced to kill.

The man cranked the device. His thinkers said the creatures must be attracted to the sound of the airship's rotators. Trunculin has written of similar problems. *But of course we are both liars*, he thought.

To the man, the sound that the device made was different than the noise of the rotators, but before he had a chance to decide if it would work, a Jhalgon fish erupted out of the water to the right of their boat. Its leathery wet wings pushed it straight up into the air. The waves made by the monster rocked his boat and the boats just twenty feet away. The beast was massive. He had read the reports and interrogated those that spotted them. But to see a sixty-foot monster lunge straight into the air was a marvel. The men were all frozen with shock. *They look more like boys than ever.*

The monster arced, and the man realized it was coming down. It opened its massive jaws to reveal its three rows of teeth. *Each tooth must be bigger than my hand ...* but his mind turned to the other boat. The seawater falling from the giant fish rained on the second boat, but they realized what was happening too late for them to get away. The monster landed on the second boat, and the beast forced the longboat under the waves before the wood snapped under the pressure.

The shock of the impact felt like a tidal wave as the two other longboats fought to stay upright. A circle of red emanated out from where the beast had gone under. Fragments of the broken longboat, no bigger than the size of a plate, floated and rode the waves. Luckily, the red was the only part they saw of their fallen friends. The rest must have gone under, or been swallowed by the beast.

The two remaining boats continued to bail the water out that had lapped over the sides. The man stood up, grasping the giant metal spear. It was longer than the man was tall, but he stood straight, feeling the cold metal slick with sea water. He stood on sure legs, riding the rocking motion, scanning for any sign of the beast.

"Fin!" A man shouted from the other boat. The man smiled until he realized it was not headed for his boat. *No, monster, come for me.* He realized what his face must look like as he glanced at the young man with the wispy beard, his face horrified and desperate. But when he saw the bare chested man looking at him, the young man's face changed to a hardy resolve. He bailed the water faster.

The fin came up from the water, parting it, standing five feet above the waves. The man cranked the machine again, imitating the sound of the rotators from the airships. The top of the beast crested the water with a gray hint of its enormous frame just under the waves. It didn't change direction, still headed for the second boat.

"Damn you!" the man shouted. "Men, row!" he commanded, as the young men rowed directly into the path of the fin. The man ignored the terror that gripped his crew, and raised the long metal spear. The three hooks came to a steely point with a rope firmly tied to the end.

Water sprayed as the boat rocked. The fin rose with the beast, and the wings threw sea water at them as the monster went up. The second boat was still its target, and the man realized it was only jumping his boat to get to the other.

The beast rose higher, using the giant wings to help arc its body. Just before it was directly over their boat, the man flung the spear at the belly of the Jhalgon. It struck the beast and the hooks went deep. The man held fast to the rope, ignoring the burn of the rope as it slid through his hands. Before his hands felt they would catch fire, he grabbed the rope firmly and was lifted off the boat.

Hurt, the beast changed its angle and missed the second boat. The beast hit the icy waters, the man following. His bare chest exploded with a thousand needles as the beast dragged him down. Already fighting for air, the man strained his muscles and forced himself to climb along the rope towards the beast. It was dragging him ever deeper, but he ignored the pressure building in his head.

Hand over hand he pulled himself along the rope until he finally reached the beast. He groped for his short knife, fearing he had lost it. One hand held the rope tightly as he fumbled to find the knife, ignoring the pains in his chest. He finally found the blade and jammed it into the beast. He jabbed again. Over and over again he stabbed at the monster while warm blood flowed past him. The beast bled as he was dragged deeper into the quickly darkening deep.

The man had done all he could. He let go of the rope and used the last of his strength to push up to the light. He had no air.

No, this is not how I die.

It was getting harder to think. The cold felt like knives going deeper and deeper, aiming for his heart. Still, he moved his legs, pushing towards the light. Just when he thought his muscles would fail him, he felt the precious air fill his lungs.

His ears were filled with the sound of water, like the sea had invaded his mind. As he took his second and third gasps of air, he finally heard the cheering. The two boats were far away from him, but the shouting was fierce.

It stopped abruptly when the beast appeared again.

The fin shot straight up out of the water, not far from the man. The man groped for his knife, but realized he had dropped it while searching for air and light. The fin bobbed up again, then slowly rolled to one side. The leathery wings splayed out on either side of the beast, which bobbed with the waves and was surrounded by the red draining from its wounds. The blood reached the man and warmed him.

The great cheers got louder and became a chant. "Father! Father! Father! Father...!"

The man smiled.

Yes, my children, let's begin this new day with blood.

Chapter 2

Visions

Firstcouncilor Trunculin and King Asa had returned from the mess they left in the kingdom of Thure. Loren and the Thurian merchant Denogg had escaped, gone without a trace. Trunculin had put Asa in his chamber under his loyal guards. They had been orders not to hurt him any further, unless Trunculin gave express permission. Better to rule the boy by fear. He knows what I'm capable of now. He won't get out from under my thumb again, Trunculin thought as he stared at the mystic.

The mystic sat in the small room, eyes closed. After all these years, Trunculin was still uneasy around them. He wondered if the feeling would ever go away. Trunculin looked back at the mystic. His eyes were open now, staring. The mystic did not speak.

After a long moment, Trunculin could not bear the silence, "Well...?" the mystic said nothing. Trunculin asked, "Why were you so hard to reach?"

The mystic answered in his own time. "I had business elsewhere. You are not the only kingdom that concerns us."

Trunculin knew this was true. He had been around long enough to see the secret hand of the mystic guild do its work. "Fair enough. When can you begin with the boy?"

The mystic stared. "I have questions."

"Questions? About what?"

The mystic Valren said, "Since Gordon collapsed, things have gone badly for you."

"That didn't sound like a question," Trunculin rubbed his forehead. The mystic stared. "Gordon and his uncle escaped. Brenddel was nearly killed tracking them down. My new alliance with Thure is gone. Then Gordon died. Then I found out Mantuan and Gordon are alive after all. But wait! Gordon has been taken, and Mantuan has stolen one of my airships. Yes, mystic, you could say I've had better times!"

The Mystic stared.

"What about the boy?" asked Trunculin.

"I am not someone you can intimidate, firstcouncilor."

"I know that," said Trunculin. "I ... I regret my tone. You and your guild have been very helpful to me. I haven't forgotten that. But how do my troubles change anything with my new boy king?"

"Because I will not help you control this king."

The words were like a slap across Trunculin's face. He managed, "How can that be your decision? You have ..."

"I know what my guild has done for you. We are turning our eyes to other matters." Valren stopped speaking, but this pause seemed different. He was not staring at the firstcouncilor, but almost through him. Trunculin had never seen the mystic behave this way.

Before Trunculin could ask if he was alright, the mystic's face changed. His features seem to melt into a mask of pain, then he screamed.

Trunculin didn't know what to do. He expected guards to rush in, but realized frantically that he never kept guards around when he saw the mystic. Trunculin put his hand out to him, but the mystic was now looking around the room like he wasn't there. He didn't scream again, just kept looking everywhere in the room, his face frantic and worried. Trunculin realized he wasn't really in the room.

He was inside a vision.

"No!" Valren shouted, but no words came out. He was standing on a ship. The sky was dark, but it was daytime. The darkness came from great black clouds. No, not clouds. They were silver and black and instead of

water, they rained destruction. So many arrows. The great kingdom was falling. All around him, waterships were sinking.

Then he was under the water. He was one of the old ones now, the Jhalgon. He was looking through the eyes of the great finned beast. And all around him the sea roiled with his siblings. He crested the water to see the other great kingdoms fall, one by one. First Artoth, then Thure. The kingdoms were all on fire. The banners with the triangle and thirteen longknives fell to the water. Two shadows appeared, as though the sun was extinguished from two different directions. He looked out through his Jhalgon eyes, to the enormous black and silver clouds that weren't clouds. But now he could see they were enormous airships, the new monsters in the world. His head split with a terrible sound he could not extinguish. And the mighty Jhalgon were afraid...

Valren was back in the small room, Trunculin's hand on his arm. Valren pulled his arm away from Trunculin's cold hand. The firstcouncilor saw the look on his face and was deeply concerned. He had never seen a mystic have a vision. "Valren, are you ...?"

The mystic seemed to recoil at the words, rubbing his arm where Trunculin had touched him. He saw the look on Trunculin's face and regained his composure. Valren's face returned to his unreadable mask. "I am fine firstcouncilor."

"What did you see?"

"I don't know..." his tone changed, "...I'm sure it was nothing. Visions happen on their own time, the reasons never immediately clear. I'm sorry you had to see it."

Trunculin began, "What was ...?"

"I must go," said Valren. "I can't help you with the new king. I have other matters I must see to."

"But, can't you at least stay for ...?"

Valren left without saying another word. He closed the door, leaving a baffled Trunculin alone. Valren walked away from the room, rubbing his arm again. *I see you now firstcouncilor*, he thought. And for the first time that Valren could remember, he felt the icy hand of fear.

Chapter 3

The Lawkeeper

"We have to go back and find him, Mantuan!" said Aline angrily. "How could this happen?"

"It is my failure, but we will find Gordon. Right now we can do nothing, there are only a handful of us. We can't go back to the kingdom of the gods against two armies and Brenddel's men. Besides, I think Gordon may have been taken to Extatumm."

"Why? What would they want with him?"

"I'm not sure. But you heard what Santovan said about people disappearing. I don't think he was taken by chance. Those young people dressed in white must work for Extatumm somehow. It could be that Extatumm wants Gordon as some sort of bargain or ransom."

"No one knew Gordon was there. No one even knows Gordon is alive, except for us."

"I'm not so sure. There was a man in a red tunic, and another man with Brenddel. The other man looked like someone I know from Thure. If the man in red was from Extatumm, maybe he had time to tell someone. But we can't just fly into Extatumm. Their army is rumored to be vast. We will rescue Gordon. But first, we have to go get the lawkeeper and convince him to come with us. Then, we go back to the fortress. We'll figure out how to rescue Gordon from there."

Aline walked back and forth, and growled with rage before she calmed, "I know you're right, Manny. I just can't stand the thought of not doing anything. Why does it feel like everything is against us?"

"Because they are. It's always easy to do the wrong thing. It's easy to destroy things and give in to darkness, like Trunculin does. It's always harder to do what is right. But we will find Gordon and we will win the war against Trunculin's evil. Now, we have a task at hand."

"I'll have to accept that … for now. But, are you sure we can reach this place even with the airship?"

"No. But I think fate owed us some good news, don't you? Somehow I feel we are supposed to find him." Santovan's maps called for them to go deep into the snowy mountains. Eventually they arrived near the location on the maps.

They could see the distant sun, but it didn't seem to make the weather any warmer. There was snow everywhere in the high mountains. It was bitterly cold and the standard uniforms and blankets stored on the airships only helped so much.

Since they had long since passed a place where any other humans lived, it was easy to spot the small trail of smoke rising from the side of the mountain. They were not close enough to see a structure or a cave, but it was obvious that someone lived there. Mantuan understood why Santovan was so negative about the lawkeeper. It wasn't finding him, it was getting to him in the steep, high mountains. The climb looked impossible without an airship.

Although Mantuan had been on many airships, it had been years. He was increasingly worried about how high they were in such cold weather. The rotators were already making stranger and stranger sounds as they climbed.

When they were close to the smoke, Mantuan looked down to see exactly how tall the mountains were. Because of the weather, he could barely see the ground at all. He looked back to where the smoke was rising and he could see a small clearing of maybe one hundred feet, in and around where the cave had to be. There was no way to land the airship, so they would have to rope down to the clearing.

"Do you think he'll be alone?" asked Lantovas.

"I'm sure he's alone. I just don't know if he'll be happy to see strangers. He must have heard us coming. Our rotators are not a natural sound. And, since he hasn't come out to greet us, I'm guessing that he may not be overly friendly," warned Mantuan. "We will have to be careful."

Aline, Lantovas, and Mantuan all carried as much protection from the cold as they could, and as many weapons as they dared.

Mantuan said, "We will rope down at the end of the clearing, and walk up so that we don't seem threatening. I don't want him to think the three of us are his enemies."

They hovered over the spot and lowered the ropes, checking for any movement. There was none, only the wind and cold. From his new angle, Mantuan thought he could see the cave entrance.

The three lowered themselves on the ropes, scanning constantly, making sure there were no arrows flying their way. Mantuan had instructed the pilot to stay as close to the mountain as they dared, and the ropes in place, so they could climb them quickly if they had to escape.

When they were firmly on the ground, Mantuan looked at the steep mountain above them. There was only a thin layer of snow above their position. There was no chance of an avalanche, so he yelled as loudly as he could. "Hello!" the word echoed throughout the mountains many times until it faded away.

No response.

They walked slowly towards the mouth of the cave. Aline pointed out that the clearing had been recently cleared of snow. There were several trees growing out of the side of the mountain, branches hanging over the clearing as they walked forward. A few times, they had to duck underneath a branch laden with fresh snow. The fact that it was not snowing at the moment helped them see ahead, as the cold sun glowed weakly through the frosty haze.

Every few feet, Mantuan yelled greetings again. Each time he got no response. They were about fifty feet from the entrance when they could see it was covered in what looked like animal skins. There were sharpened sticks coming out of the ground near the cave and all around the entrance. Apparently, the lawkeeper did not want visitors.

They ducked under another tree branch, and even though they heard no sound, something fell onto Lantovas' back. At first it looked like a large chunk of snow had fallen on him, but as it moved they could tell it was a snowcat.

"Ahhggg!" Lantovas tried to throw the large cat off as it clawed his back. The cat tried to sink its teeth into his neck, but Lantovas rolled on his back and on top of the snowcat. It didn't release its grip. He pulled his shortknife, but could not get at the attacking cat.

Lantovas tried to crush the animal with his own weight, and Mantuan and Aline had their knives out. Aline tried to stab at it, but the cat and Lantovas were rolling around on the snow. She was afraid she would stab the guard.

Someone came out of nowhere, dressed in white furs. The figure leaped to Lantovas, sliding a shortknife deep into the cat's neck, which immediately went limp. Lantovas slumped with a groan, red blood flowing over the white snow. The fur-covered figure said, "Get him inside. I need to attend to these wounds."

Mantuan took quick action, putting the man over his shoulder. Lantovas was in a great deal of pain as they stepped around the sharpened sticks and walked through the skins covering the opening.

In the cave, the figure threw off the white furs. "Put him face down on the table."

Mantuan froze, his heart nearly stopped.

"It can't be," said Mantuan, getting to one knee. "My queen. I ... I thought you were dead."

The woman ripped off Lantovas' coat and shirt to expose his wounds. She was already putting some sort of sticky cream on his cuts. "That's strange, Mantuan. I thought *you* died on an airship with my husband. Get off your knee, I'm not a queen anymore."

"Arrggh!" screamed Lantovas as she applied the cream.

"Sorry, this is going to hurt. But without it, those scratches won't heal and they will become infected. Cats may lick themselves, but that doesn't make them clean," said the queen, continuing to put the sticky gray paste on the man's wounds.

"Why do animals keep attacking me?" moaned Lantovas.

"You must taste good," offered Aline. Lantovas tried to laugh, but apparently that made it hurt more.

"I like her," the queen said, working quickly with her healing paste. "As much as I want to know why you're alive, Mantuan, I'd rather know why you're here. You have an airship – are you Trunculin's friend again?" She turned her head to glare at him.

"I was never Trunculin's friend. We stole the airship from Brenddel," said Mantuan.

She returned her attention to Lantovas. "Good. I hope you killed that monster."

"I started to, but he ran to get more men."

"Too bad. But I'm sure there will be another chance. Monsters always come back. Come here and help me, girl."

"Aline," she said, coming to help.

"Okay Aline, we need to turn him over. The cat scratched above his chest, too. It's going to hurt him as we turn him over. Mantuan, I need your help too."

Lantovas said, "I am right here, you know." they turned him and Lantovas yelled as he was placed gently on his back. She put more healing paste on his wounds and healing cloth over that. The woman gave him something, and Lantovas was soon sleeping off the pain.

The queen made some tea. She gave a second pot to Aline to have brought up to the airship. "My cave is too small for more people, but there's no reason for them to freeze to death up there," she said. She sent her with a torch. "The cats hate fire and bright light. You should be safe out there for now."

Aline left the cave. The woman said, "What does the girl know? Can we speak openly?"

"Yes." said Mantuan.

The queen slapped Mantuan hard across the face.

"Why did you let him die? You were supposed to protect him!"

"I deserve that. And more. Many times I wished I had died that day, instead of Daymer. I should have died for failing my king, your husband. I am sorry."

The queen came to him and hugged him this time. He hugged her back.

"I'm sorry Mantuan. I've just been trying to forget how it all went wrong. And now here you are, back from the dead. What happened that day? I only know the story from one point of view."

"I still don't know exactly what lies Trunculin put in Brenddel's head. But I assume he told him that you and the king were responsible for the slavery at the gas fields. I was looking over the railing at something. To this day, I can't remember what. And when I turned around, Brenddel had stabbed the king and pushed him over. I was on the other side of the deck. I ran, but the king had already fallen. We battled, but whatever Trunculin had told Brenddel fueled him with rage and strength. I have never seen him fight so hard, and he was nearly as good as me without the rage."

"He was your adopted son, of course he was strong," said the queen.

"Yes, well, that was a long time ago. I know my love for him was why I let my guard down. I went over the edge and fell through a canopy of trees. As fate would have it, there were people living in the trees. A whole little village."

"That's amazing. I know you believed in gods once. Did that strengthen your faith?"

"A little, yes." replied Mantuan.

Aline slowly come back in, "Is it alright? I could go back to the ship if you like…"

The queen responded, "No, no. Come have some tea and tell me how you know this big, one eyed warrior."

Aline smiled. "Manny? Oh, he's not that tough. You should see him play with a litter of puppies."

"That was one time. And you know not to call me that."

The queen said, "Sounds like you've known each other for a long time, Manny."

"Manny is the father I never knew. When he literally fell into my life, I was just a little girl. My mother wasn't there. I think we adopted each other. My village is a band of people looking for a better place, far up in the trees."

"How do you live in the trees, exactly?" asked the queen.

"Same way you live far up in a mountain, I guess. But, with better weather."

"I definitely like her," said the queen.

"We have the forest nearly all to ourselves. Over the years there were rumors spread that the forest is haunted. Mantuan has helped keep that legend alive with some secrets we found there. Every time someone is running from something and finds our forest, they enter and never leave. That's how we grow our village."

Mantuan agreed. "We have a very good security system. That forest is haunted, by us. Plenty of fresh water and game. We grow and hunt all our own food. We call it the fortress. And you, my queen? Why hide up here?"

"I'm not hiding. This is my home now. You answer my questions first. If you didn't know I was alive, why are you here?" asked the queen.

"We were looking for the lawkeeper. I had no idea it would be you."

"What do you know of the lawkeeper?" asked the queen.

"We heard for years, in many kingdoms, that there was someone going through old records and documents. Scouring our world for something. I tracked you for years, but I was always just behind you," said Mantuan.

"That was you? By the gods, I thought it was Trunculin or his agents," said the queen. "I have learned how to hide myself very well after the world thought I was dead."

"There are a lot of people coming back from the dead lately." added Aline.

Mantuan said, "I found out that what this lawkeeper was looking for was original laws. Laws having to do with the kingdom of the thirteen, and outsider accounts of our kingdom in the early days, but especially anything written about the first thirteen."

The queen nodded. "And do you know why I was looking and collecting?"

"I think you realized that Trunculin has been destroying our kingdom's first laws quietly. I think you found proof."

"I did. Follow me."

She led them to another room in the naturally formed cave. The queen pulled back a curtain to reveal an alcove in the wall. There was a table with stacks of books, papers, and scrolls. Many of them looked very old.

"I wanted some privacy, but it appeared my cave is also a perfect place to protect documents from crumbling into dust. You don't know how long I spent in dusty old rooms. In Thure alone, I must have gone down a mile or more - five thousand feet under the ground. There is a vast kingdom under Thure, full of papers and other things. I was even able to get into Extatumm without the council or their agents knowing. I looked through many of the old documents from Dard, the ones they didn't destroy."

"I had no idea it would be this much," said Mantuan.

"What you also don't know is why I started looking," said the queen, pulling out a small drawer. "I found this in a lower level, in a secret hiding place in the palace. Do you remember when the king and I got married and that I helped restored the palace? Well, I found this myself, hidden in a wall. It is an original law book." The queen handed the book to Mantuan and said, "Very carefully, look at the first page."

Mantuan opened the book carefully and read the inside cover. "Borenn. This belonged to our first king?"

"Yes. You have no idea what's in this original material I found. It proves Trunculin has changed the law completely. Our kingdom is nearly upside down from what it should be."

Mantuan smiled. "This is exactly what I'm looking for, to expose Trunculin for what he is."

The queen took the book from Mantuan's hands and put it back in the drawer. "It makes no difference. You asked me why I hide up here. It's not just to preserve the documents. It doesn't matter if you passed these documents out on the streets of the kingdom to every person. No one would know what it truly meant, because Trunculin has succeeded in changing history. No one can comprehend how his lies have taken root in the people. What can be done now? Trunculin has already won."

"My queen, this man has taken everything from you. Your husband, your kingdom, and soiled your reputation by smearing the evil of slavery on your good name. Of course you feel that way," said Mantuan.

Aline added, "We can't let Trunculin win. He must be brought down in the full light of day, his evil exposed to everyone. Who better to do it than you?"

The queen responded. "Who would believe a slaver queen? That is what he convinced them of, didn't he? Before I saw it with my own eyes, I would not have believed what was in these documents. But simply showing old documents will prove nothing."

Aline said, "We have a small army of people helping us gather other proof. But we also have Gordon. When we restore him as king, it will be a powerful symbol..."

"What do you mean Gordon?"

"Loren has raised him to be a fine young man, my queen. With the documents and Gordon, we will defeat Trunculin," said Mantuan.

Queen Ellice froze. "Are you telling me that my brother and my son are still alive?"

Chapter 4

Gordon's First Ride

Gordon's sight was just returning. Through a gray haze of dim lights and colors, he tried to focus. Darkly colored, blurry figures were moving around far off in the distance. He blinked furiously to clear his vision and tried to remember what happened. Those girls in white. *The powder must have been something to make me sleep.*

He was laying on a rope bed with a small blanket over his legs. His eyes had finally started to clear enough to see he was tied to the bed. *But where am I?* From the scenery going by, he realized that he must be in the air. But if he was on an airship, was he going back to Trunculin?

His heart sank as he realized that must be the truth. Only his kingdom had airships, and Trunculin must have had agents in Artoth to capture him. He wondered if he was the only prisoner onboard. *I finally get to ride on an airship, and it's taking me to my death.*

He looked at his hands, which were bound with metal shackles. He moved his hands and found that they weren't very tight. He stretched his neck and looked all around. He could only see two men talking near the front of the ship.

He wiggled his wrists and found that he could take the shackles off easily. He supposed they were not meant for a thirteen year old, or they might have thought he would be asleep longer. From the front of the deck he heard, "Go check on him. See if he's awake."

Gordon froze. He didn't know if he would have time to get his hands back through the shackles, so he put his hands in the same position and put the small blanket back over his hands. He kept his eyelids open just a tiny bit as the man stood over him. Gordon tried to control his breathing as though he was still asleep. The man stood there a moment and walked off. "He's still out," the man said to the other.

"Good. I don't want to deal with some brat who thinks he's a king," and both men laughed. Gordon untied himself from the rope bed and got up slowly and carefully, grateful that his legs had not been tied. He checked his belt and found he still had his weapons. Both longknife and short were there. *I'm being guarded by careless men*, he thought.

He knew that any airship would have more than two men in their crew. As he cautiously looked around, something was wrong. This looked like no airship he had ever seen. Naturally, airships were highly guarded secrets. They didn't let just anyone get close to them. But Gordon has seen them flying many times around his kingdom, studying every detail when he could. Even from on deck, where he had never been before, he could tell that something was not quite right.

First, he noticed that it was too small, painted strangely, not anything like his kingdom's colors. And everywhere he looked there was random items: bags of sweet salt, grain, and large rolls of clothing. It looked like the hold of a watership that did trading. Traders often had small crews. Maybe this ship had only a few men onboard after all.

There were also no lanterns. There were a few arrow guns with large arrows, but no other weapons like the fire weapons; the kind by which Gordon had almost been killed once. He glanced at the men up front, who were still looking forward. Gordon was near the back of the ship. He knew he couldn't take two grown men on his own. He could only think of one thing he could do, but he would have to time it very carefully.

The two men were up front and jesting about the girls in white. "I wish they had stayed when they dropped off the boy. They would have been better company than you," said the man piloting the ship.

The other man said, "They wouldn't give an ugly dog like you a second glance ... is something wrong?"

The man said, "We're losing height. Strange ..." the man said, looking around, "Hey!"

He spotted Gordon at the back of the ship, standing on the railing, reaching up to the floating section of the ship. Being spotted, Gordon worked faster, using his longknife to slowly slice through the airship's rear floating section. He could feel the air escaping quickly as the airship lost more height.

The pilot stayed at the wheel, while the other man came running for Gordon. As he approached, he shouted, "Wake up!" Gordon saw the heads of three men pop up from near where he had been on the rope bed. Gordon realized that there were other men aboard after all. They had just been napping. His situation just got even more dangerous.

Gordon cut faster.

The pilot shouted back, "Stop him *now*, we're losing too much air... you two! Start throwing things overboard. We won't clear the gates."

Gordon stopped cutting, hearing what the pilot had said. He didn't want his first airship ride to fall from the sky. He thought if it sank slowly enough, he might be able to get close enough to the ground to jump off. That seemed more and more unlikely.

The first man reached him. As the man reached for him, Gordon jumped down off the railing. Gordon slashed his longknife at the man. The curved blade connected with his calf and the man went down, screaming with surprise.

Others were fast approaching, and they all drew their knives when they saw the boy attack. Gordon hadn't really thought of what he would do next. He looked around and noticed that the ship was headed straight for a large gate. It was enormous. He knew the pilot could not get more lift with all the gas escaping. A few men were throwing things overboard, but they were still sinking.

Two more men were almost to Gordon, who sheathed his longknife and dove for the railing. He grabbed for the rope hanging there, as the man closest to him shouted, "No!"

Gordon was over the railing, hanging from the rope. He doubted the men would cut his rope and let Gordon fall, but he had a bigger problem. The large gate was surrounded by sheer mountain cliffs.

Gordon struggled to stay on the rope as the airship lost height and veered towards the mountainside. He was nearly flung against the jutting rocks and small trees growing out of the cliff wall. He slowly and painfully made his way down the rope, while one of the men climbed down his own rope about six feet from Gordon's. The man was being swung around wildly, "Fool boy, climb back up…"

Before he could finish his thought, the man's rope hit the mountain and an outcropped tree caught him. The rope went slack with the man no longer on it. Gordon was not close enough to the ground to let go. They were still at least fifty feet in the air, and the airship was going down so quickly, that he would have been killed even if his feet touched the ground.

The ship was dropping faster, and Gordon wondered if he should have stayed onboard after all. The airship came close to the mountain again and Gordon saw the tree before he hit it. He grabbed for the leaves, and let go of the rope. It was no use, he realized. He lost his grip and started tumbling through small trees and brush, down the steep mountain.

Chapter 5

The Two Kings

"Will they be much longer?" asked Brenddel of the blue guard.

"The king is a busy man. He does not work on your schedule," said the guard, "just be honored he has agreed to see you at all."

Brenddel turned his attention to the other guard on the orange side of the room. "And your king? Any word on how long he might be?"

The other guard said, "My king never takes an audience until the blue king arrives."

Brenddel tried to control his anger. One of the thing he hated most was waiting on others when he had things to do. He thought that finding his airship, killing Mantuan again, and finding out what Trunculin was up to, formed a pretty important list.

More than anything, he hated politics.

Another hour passed before a large group of people came through the king's blue door. There were at least twenty people that arrived ahead of him. A few of them stayed near the king's chair, but most of them went out into the larger room, chatting and milling around.

The guards opened the other, orange door. The same thing happened, with more people filling the room. Somewhere a loud musical gong sound vibrated through the room. Brenddel had been told how much ceremony there was involved in the kingdom of the gods. *I'm lucky I left when I was a boy. At least I avoided all this waste of time,* Brenddel thought to himself.

A young man came out of each king door and loudly announced their ruler. They did this at the same exact time, so that Brenddel couldn't understand what they were saying. They were talking over each other and each man got louder as his presentation went on. He assumed they were both announcing the arrival of their own king. Sure enough, both kings walked out at exactly the same time.

Almost.

Brenddel noticed, as they both stepped into the room. The orange king paused for just a moment so that the blue king was actually in the room first. *By the gods, they're acting like children*, Brenddel thought. Both kings looked straight ahead as they sat in their chairs, not looking at each other.

A man standing next to the blue king said, "My king Ninnith of the kingdom of the gods of Artoth, high priest of the pact with man, bids you welcome, most humbly."

A man standing next to the orange king said, "My king Tethon, son of Torr the magnificent, king of Artoth and high ruler of the gods of punishment, offers welcome to these worthy visitors."

"Who's in charge of this attack?" said the blue king on the left.

The orange king on the right said, "Please ask the other king if he is sure it was an attack." the man next to him repeated what he said to the other king.

The blue king responded, "Tell the orange king that my reports confirm that there was a battle. Tell the other king that we know he knows this. They were his men after all."

Neither king looked directly at the other.

Brenddel began to speak, "I am the..."

"Come forward and stand on that circle. Yes, the one on the floor there," said the blue king.

"You will speak to both of us, looking forward, never looking directly in our eyes," said the orange king.

Brenddel had the sudden urge to jump between them and punch them equally in the face. He resisted this urge and carefully stood on the circle, looked forward and said, "Kings of Artoth, let me first say that I meant no disrespect to either of you personally, nor any of your people. I am on a mission from my king to find two men. Men that we believe poisoned the king of Thure. While searching, I saw a man that I thought was dead. We fought."

"Who is this man?" said the blue king.

Brenddel hesitated for a moment and said, "His name is Mantuan."

The crowd was suddenly paying attention. There were whispers and gasps throughout the crowds.

"We remember Mantuan. He fought with us in the war of Asgonan that spilled blood in our good kingdom. You say that he is alive and here in our kingdom?" said the king on the right.

Brenddel started to look at the king. The blue king warned him to keep looking forward. Brenddel complied reluctantly. "Yes, he is alive. And he was in your kingdom. Before he stole my airship and fled."

This caused laughter and chatter in the room.

"Yes, we… we heard about that," said the blue king, barely containing a smile.

"With your permission, Kings of Artoth, I would like to hire a watership and get my men back to my own kingdom."

"And who will pay for my men?" asked the orange king, barring his sharpened teeth.

"I don't understand," said Brenddel.

"Who will pay for my dead soldiers? Their burials? Make amends to their families?" the orange king asked.

"None of my men touched your soldiers," said Brenddel, who was beginning to lose his patience. "That was Mantuan."

"You are speaking to the king of mighty Artoth. You will watch your tone," warned a man standing next to the blue king.

"My apologies. But, Mantuan killed your men. Take it up with him, if you can find him," Brenddel said, trying hard to control his tone of voice.

The orange king barred his sharpened teeth again and said, "I am taking the matter up with you."

"My airship is gone. I couldn't pay you even if I wanted to, since all the coin I had is on my ship. And I can't go and retrieve my ship until I leave your kingdom and get another airship to find him."

The orange king sounded concerned. "You have no coin to make amends?"

Brenddel clarified, "I am saying there are no amends to make. I am not responsible for what Mantuan has done. And yes, I'm saying there is no coin. I will have to find a ship that will take me to my kingdom to be paid when we get there."

The king on the left said wearily, "I see. The matter is clear then. Does the other king understand and agree?"

The orange king replied, "Yes I do, if the other king also agrees."

"Agreed," said the blue king.

The king on the right looked directly at Brenddel and said, "If there is no way to pay this debt, blood demands blood."

A look of confusion crossed Brenddel's face, until he heard the commotion behind him. Four of the orange guards quickly stepped forward and opened the throats of four of Brenddel's men. There was no time to defend themselves. The four men dropped to the floor, dead.

There were gasps from some of the guests while others actually clapped their hands, as though they had just seen a performance.

Brenddel and his men quickly drew their longknives and formed a circle, with their knives facing outward to protect every man. None of the guards from either king made any attempt to attack them.

"You are mad, both of you. My men were innocent!" said Brenddel.

"No one is innocent," said the blue king.

"The gods must be paid," said the orange king, bearing his sharpened teeth again.

"We would have preferred the coin, of course," said the blue king.

Brenddel and his men stood in formation. Brenddel asked, "So, what happens now?"

"You are free to go," said the blue king.

"Since you have no coin to bury your men, you will have to take the bodies with you. We will not charge you for cleaning up the mess," said the orange king.

Brenddel wanted nothing more than to leap onto the platform and kill both kings right there. But since he had no easy way to escape, he decided against it. *I suppose Trunculin might be a little annoyed if I did*, he thought darkly.

Brenddel said, "Sheath your knives and stand down," and his men did. Brenddel and his men started to carry the bodies outside.

In unison this time, the men standing at each king's side said, "Stranger to this land, you will show the kings of Artoth the proper respect."

Brenddel stopped. The murderous urge came over him again. He turned around and walked slowly to the circle on the floor, his hand firmly on the hilt of his longknife.

He bent ever so slightly at his waist to the king on the left, giving the smallest bow he could. He did the same to the king on the right, looking directly in the king's face. Both kings had turned their heads to face forward and did not acknowledge him.

Brenddel walked out with his men, both the living and the dead.

Chapter 6

The Father

Gordon was standing on an airship, but something was wrong. He looked around. From this height, he couldn't tell which kingdom was below. It was burning. He looked at the waters below and they looked like they were boiling. Everywhere there was the smell of smoke and fire. Airships were exploding out of the skies all around. He thought he might be dreaming, but then he felt two hands close around his throat, squeezing. *Can you feel pain in a dream?* He thought wildly, and tried to pry the hands away, but they were too strong. He felt his own neck snap, then someone threw him from the airship.

Gordon eyes shot open and he raised his head off the pillow. He felt for his throat, but that's not where the pain was coming from. The real pain made him put his hand on the back of his head. His wound screamed at him as he touched it, but he couldn't remember why it hurt. He laid his aching head back down, blinked a few times, and realized he was in a large bedroom. There were blankets over him and pillows behind him. They were soft and warm.

Despite the pain, he forced himself to sit up. He was in soft bed clothing as well. He thought as hard as he could to remember why he was here. Then he remembered the real airship, the cliff, and falling. He had no idea how he'd survived.

He wondered briefly if he was dead, but the throbbing pain in his head made him doubt it. This was the third time recently that he had woken up in surprise or pain. He did not like that at all. He also had no idea where he was. *How many times will I wake up in strange places?* Gordon thought.

Before he could get up to look out the window, a man came in with a small tray. "Ah, you are awake. That is good. I hope you slept well, Gordon." said the man.

Gordon responded, "You know my name. Who are you? Where am I? Why was I brought here?"

The man smiled, but did not answer his questions. "Would you like some tea?"

The man had a beard and was dressed in a plain gray shirt and pants. *Strangely kind smile*, Gordon thought, but he needed answers. "Why am I here?"

"Direct. I like that. My name is TrTorrin. Many people here call me the father. I am the leader of the people's inner council. I wanted to make sure you are safe. From what I understand, there was a large group of guards headed to arrest you, maybe even to kill you. Artoth is a treacherous place."

"So you had people knock me out and bring me here by force?"

He laughed. "No, no. the girls feel terrible about it, but when they startled you, you turned and hit the back of your head on a low archway. The girls wanted to get you to the best healers."

Gordon began, "Wait...but..."

"You hit your head very hard. You were asleep for many hours. Since the airship, you have been asleep for much longer than that."

"So where...?"

"You are in Extatumm."

"That large gate. Were those the Gates of Dard I saw?"

TrTorrin laughed, "We don't call them that anymore, but yes."

"Why bring me all this way just to be healed? That makes no sense."

"We have the finest healers anywhere. The healers in the kingdom of the gods use methods from a hundred years ago. We use all the most modern techniques. I would never trust you to them, they might have killed you with their ancient ways. To that point, my healers tell me that you have the sweetblood sickness. They have done the best they can for you. We found the metal case full of medicine … medicine bread, I suppose? Do many in your kingdom have this sickness?"

Gordon was uncomfortable. "No. It's rare. My… our healers has invented some new ways to control it."

TrTorrin nodded, "they must be very good healers. To be a fine, healthy thirteen-year old with the sweetblood …"

"Am I a prisoner?" Gordon asked, changing the subject.

He laughed softly. "No, son. You are my guest. We wouldn't heal you and then keep you prisoner. We could punish you for damaging our airship, of course. I lost five good men. But since you had no idea what was going on, you were simply protecting yourself. It is only because of our healer's skills that you survived your injuries. We will keep your weapons and longknife safe. It's a lovely replica by the way."

"If I'm not a prisoner, I can just leave then?" Gordon started to get out of bed.

"Of course. But if I may ask, where would you like to go?" asked Tr-Torrin, sipping his tea. He looked at Gordon with piercing eyes. Kind, but intense. Maybe dangerous, Gordon decided. Gordon had no immediate answer.

TrTorrin continued, "I mean, you were about to be arrested in one kingdom, another kingdom thinks you poisoned their king, and your own kingdom calls you a traitor. Most of the world thinks you are dead. And there has been no one contacting us to find you. It seems your friends are not looking for you. So, where would you like to go?"

Gordon knew that this man had secret reasons for wanting him and that he was lying about the girls and hitting his head, too. But this man was also right. His friends had no idea where he was and everyone else thought he was dead.

"Perhaps we could contact your friends for you. If you would just give me their names and where we can send the message." he said, pulling out a small notebook and pen.

Gordon knew he couldn't name his friends, since the world still thought Mantuan was dead. But he also knew that he had no idea where his friends were, and he wouldn't tell this man even if he did know.

"No? I certainly understand loyalty and friendship," he said as he put his note pad away. "Maybe you could be our guest until we figure everything out?"

Gordon didn't know what else to do. "I suppose I have no choice. Oh, and thank you for ..." as he touched the back of his head.

"No trouble," TrTorrin said getting up. "There are men just outside the door in case you need anything. Please don't hesitate to ask."

"I will ... um ... thank you, TrTor..." said Gordon.

"TrTorrin. Goodbye for now, Gordon," said the man as he left the room.

TrTorrin informed the guards outside the door that Gordon was not to leave under any circumstances, and to send word to him directly if the boy asked for anything. The man seated outside Gordon's room got up with a book in his arm and followed the father.

"How is the boy?" asked Coltun, the father's assistant. He no longer wore the red cloak he had in Artoth. Now his small, slim shape wore a gray outfit much like the father's.

The father replied, "He is fine. He understands his position. He should be easy to control. How are negotiations going with this...?"

"Darion," said Coltun, "they seem to be going well. His motivations still make me a bit nervous. I think he has other plans he's not telling us. But he might be an unexpected ally."

"What is the report on the fleet?" asked the father.

"Ship fifty seven is almost ready. We've been doing some extra testing of our newer airships as we discussed, near the outlands. No one seems to have noticed us, or cares that we are there."

"Maybe we should turn our attention to exploring, instead of conquest. The outlands are mysterious, tempting." said the father.

"We may want to focus on who we take down after Artoth. With an ally in Darion, we may not need to destroy Thure at all. If we could lend him help in overthrowing the queen, we may be able to control him. Control Thure instead of destroying it."

"We shall see. Destroying the kingdom of the gods must be our first step. It will certainly be the most rewarding. What about the missing airships?"

Coltun paused before saying, "That is the most troubling thing. Five are now missing."

"Five? I thought there were three missing."

"It was three until yesterday. This time two went missing in one day. One of our men was found this time, dead in the waters near the outer banks. We think a watership is being used somehow. I still think we should alert all of the pilots."

"No," said the father firmly. "I will not have anyone on the outer council finding out about this. I have already had to put down two challenges to my leadership. I will not give them anything to use against me."

"Yes, father."

"And find out where they are hiding my ships. Five airships can't just disappear," said the father. "Where's Darion now? I'd like to meet him."

Coltun replied, "This way, father."

Chapter 7

Stories of the Dead

The airship was fully loaded, the crew having packed the last of the ancient papers collected by Queen Ellice, also known as the lawkeeper. They were soon underway and the queen watched from the back of the ship. Her cave got smaller and smaller, until she could no longer see it at all.

"Are you sad to leave it behind, my queen?" asked Aline, trying to understand how the queen must be feeling.

"Sad to be coming back into this dark world. I thought I'd left it behind forever. I didn't think there was anything that could have brought me back." replied the queen.

Mantuan had plotted the course to the fortress and given control of the airship back to the pilot. Lantovas was feeling much better, thanks to the queen's healing skills. He stayed on deck next to the pilot. Being from Thure, he couldn't get enough of flying on an airship, and he insisted he was feeling well enough to be in the open air.

Mantuan joined Aline and Queen Ellice in the back part of the ship as they spoke of the past.

Aline said, "Loren had always told me, all of us, that you were dead."

"I can understand how he thought that. I was sure he was dead too, along with my son. My brother Loren worked at the palace as a healer. He was just one among a dozen. No one knew he was my brother, not even Trunculin. Only I and the king knew. It was only by chance that Loren was the healer chosen to be on the airship that day. That horrible day."

"I'm so sorry I couldn't protect him," said Mantuan.

The queen put her hand on his. "It was supposed to be the happiest day. Loren had done some tests in secret and confirmed that I was pregnant with Gordon. The king had always wanted a son. He insisted that if we ever had a girl he would love her just as much, but I was going to tell him the happy news that day when they returned. But then Loren came back and told me what happened. Brenddel made all the men on the airship swear they'd keep quiet, or be killed. They would've killed Loren that day too, if they knew he was my brother. I never trusted Trunculin. But when Loren came to me, I just couldn't believe he would be so bold. I will never know why Trunculin didn't have me killed the moment the airship landed, but Loren and I escaped later that day." the queen paused, still looking backward out of the airship.

Aline said, "You don't have to tell us if you don't want to."

The queen replied, "I just realized I've never told this to anyone. I want to talk about it. Loren and I finally made our way to a small cabin by a river that our parents had owned. Gordon was born there. It was old, but secluded, and we knew no one would bother us. We were wrong, of course."

"Trunculin found you," offered Mantuan.

"Of course he did. It took him over a year. But one day, I heard the airship coming, and it was too late to escape. We were going to eat our meal outside that day. Loren, myself, and my newborn son. It began as a beautiful day. Loren was with Gordon in the cabin, always good with him when he was making a fuss. I was laying out the blanket for our meal.

The airship wasted no time and dropped its fire. I had just enough time to get to my feet and jump in the river. The airship aimed the fire at the water first, and it got so hot I nearly boiled. I've got terrible burns on my back to show for that day. I thought I was trapped, but the current was strong and I was able to swim away, unseen."

"And the airship went for the cabin next," said Mantuan.

"Yes. As the current took me, I mostly stayed under the water, but I did surface just long enough to see the cabin engulfed in the fire. I almost gave up then. I started to let myself sink to the bottom, but then I let my fury keep me alive."

Aline asked, "You never saw them again?"

"No. I went back a few days later to see if somehow they had survived, but there was nothing but ashes. How *did* they survive?"

"He told me that they were in the cellar getting mushrooms. He had to dig his way out that night, from under the wreckage. They left, but Loren was convinced that the airship didn't know if anyone was inside the cabin. He thinks they burned it to erase any trace of you, my queen. You said that no one knew you were related. No one even knew you were pregnant with Gordon."

"And after surviving that nightmare. Why did Loren go back to the palace?" asked the queen.

"He hadn't intended to. He and Gordon survived, but they had nothing. The two traveled through many different villages. They stayed out of major cities. Every village he went to, he helped the people with his healing arts. By this time, I had sent out my agents over many kingdoms, secretly looking for people that could aid our cause. I was even going around and investigating myself," said Mantuan.

Ellice asked, "You were secretly back in our kingdom?"

Mantuan replied, "Yes, and I even visited the palace city a few times. I had heard about a healer in a village that was using zoress bread. Since the only person I knew that used it was Loren, I found him. We were both surprised to find each other. He told me everything that happened and I told him what I was doing. He thought it was too risky to go back to the palace city and I agreed, thinking we could work better from the villages."

"That's when king Adinn fell sick," offered Aline.

"Yes. The king was only on his third trial when he fell gravely ill. He was a smart boy, learned very quickly, and the people liked him. So naturally, Trunculin decided to bring every healer to the palace and try to heal the king. Loren had no choice. He was known in the villages, and his presence at the palace would have been missed. Each healer received an hour to examine the king and try to treat him. Loren looked at the boy for only a few moments. He could tell the boy was being poisoned, so he used his special bread to draw out the poison. The boy was fully healed within days. When Trunculin realized it was Loren, he must have been furious. But, since the king was saved and there were lots of people around, Trunculin had to take Loren back. Loren even fell to his knees and dramatically begged Trunculin for forgiveness. He told Trunculin he panicked and fled that day, then realized that he should have stayed. Trunculin may not have believed him, but Loren was a hero. Loren was made Firsthealer," explained Mantuan.

The queen responded, "That must have hurt for the Firstcouncilor."

"Maybe, but Trunculin found a way to dismiss Loren a few months later, without the public noticing. Loren was too famous to kill by then. He went back to healing in the villages. That's where Gordon was raised, in a village not too far from the palace. Loren realized that he had to keep them in public to protect himself and Gordon. So they both hid in plain sight."

"I find out my son and my brother are still alive. But one is in prison, and one has been taken." said queen Ellice.

Aline offered, "They are still alive, my queen. We will get them both back."

"First, we have to get to the fortress," said Mantuan.

"Where will you hide the airship? Won't they be looking for it?" asked queen Ellice.

Aline and Mantuan smiled at each other.

"The fortress has many secrets. It will be fine. We will see if anyone has word about Gordon or Loren," said Mantuan confidently.

"I will not lose them again Mantuan."

"Let's go to the front of the ship. You have been too long without hope. It's time to start looking forward."

Chapter 8

The Great Statue

Gordon had been looking around his room. On the walls there were three curious poems. They were all done in a beautiful handwritten script and had elaborate frames. The first one read:

Do you recall, my brother?
The bird as it flew over the gate of the king,
As first light broke in this far land,
A new wind brought the bird.
The great eye watched over us all,
It was a new day, full of promises
Do you recall?

Gordon had read the three poems several times, while being stuck in his room. He had looked out the window. It didn't open, of course, he had checked. So, he kept re-reading the poems. There was something strange and a little disturbing about them, but he kept reading them anyway. Two of them were in his bedroom, and one was hanging in his bathroom.

We will tie the whale
With our long rope.
A rainbow joins us
Where the five rivers meet.

We will slice them,
Share them with all.
The whale, we shall eat.

A knock came at the door. "Come in," said Gordon.

TrTorrin entered with a large smile. "Are you ready for the tour?" he asked brightly. "I can't wait to show you around our glorious city."

Gordon said, "I was just reading the poems here in my room. Do you know what they mean?"

"I have told them to take down those silly things. Yes, I know what they mean because I wrote them. They are printed and given out on special occasions to the people by the outer councils. I wrote them back when we were fighting to free our lands," said the father, "They are terrible, aren't they?"

"I find this one the most confusing," Gordon said, pointing to the last framed poem.

Wind and smoke swirl,
The sun is dying.
We who feel are here.
The gods marvel at the new world
As they die.
Our hearts burst as one,
When we are inches from the sky.

The father said, "I wouldn't put too much meaning into my terrible poetry. They were all written before our transformation into Extatumm. Shall we go, son?"

Gordon noticed he had not answered his questions again. He decided not to push too much, but rather watch the father, to study how he avoided answering questions.

"Yes, I'm ready," said Gordon as he checked his new clothes. They had furnished him with a new wardrobe that seem to fit exactly. He was concerned that the new wardrobe meant that he would be here a while. "Do I need to bring anything?"

TrTorrin said, "Only your medicine, just in case. How long have you had the sweetblood illness? My healers are fascinated. How does your uncle make those little medicine cakes?"

Gordon didn't want to tell this man anything, but since he really didn't know how Loren made them, he knew he could tell the truth without giving away any secrets. "I've had it since I was seven. I don't really know how he makes them. He's told me a little, but it's confusing. Something to do with a liquid he gets from animals and bakes them into the cakes for when my blood gets too sweet. He adds something so the stomach absorbs the liquid instead of breaking it down. I … I really don't feel comfortable talking about it."

TrTorrin nodded. "I see. It's a personal matter. I am always curious about things that I don't know. But no matter. Let's go, there is much to show you," said TrTorrin as he cheerfully ushered Gordon out of the room.

There was a man who looked like a councilor waiting for them. "This is my assistant Coltun. I hope you don't mind, but there are always matters to attend to. If he comes with us on the tour, it will be easier for me to get work done while I enjoy showing you around."

"It is a pleasure," said the assistant, never taking his eyes off Gordon. He kept expecting Coltun to say something else, but he didn't. He just stared at Gordon. They started their tour and Gordon found out where he had been staying. It used to be the Imperial Palace when it was the Kingdom of Dard. It was one of the only old buildings he could see.

"How much of the old Dard kingdom still exists? Do you still have the crown jewels?" asked Gordon innocently.

"My boy!" Coltun said, looking around. "We do not use that word…"

"You must forgive my assistant. He is not used to dealing with kings." the father smiled at the assistant, and Gordon noticed the assistant did not look comforted, but worried instead. "We believe in looking forward. The past is past and what is done is done. Dard, the word that you referred to, the kingdom that used to be here, is actually forbidden in Extatumm. There's just no use talking about the past, you understand."

"Sorry. I just always loved history and studied the kings and queens of Dar..." Gordon quickly caught himself and continued, "...of the kingdom that used to be here. My uncle always said that we should learn from the past."

The father said, "Your uncle sounds like a wise man. Education is extremely important in every aspect of life. I, myself, have studied the histories of all the kingdoms. The thing about history is that you must learn all your lessons, and then move on and close the book. Learning from the past is one thing, but dwelling in the past is something entirely different."

Gordon thought about that and something about it bothered him, but he wasn't sure what it was.

"Speaking of history. This is the statue of our founder. The great man. Ollander Adair, our most important thinker."

Gordon asked, "He had two names?"

"Yes, strange, I know. He was from another land. Their gods require two names when a man is born," said the father.

Gordon looked at the giant statue. It was a glimmering statue of a man standing with one hand behind him, and the other hand was above his head in a kind of salute, or maybe as though he was trying to look into the distance. It was obvious the man had a beard, but Gordon couldn't quite understand what was happening at the top of the statue.

"I see you are confused by the head of the great man," said the father looking upward and looking back at Gordon. "You must forgive me, Gordon, but we don't allow a lot of visitors into our kingdom since we're still so misunderstood. I can see, looking at it from your perspective, how strange it must look. As you can see, the man has the outline of a head. It shows his great formal beard, but the statue was made so that you could clearly see inside the great thinker's mind and beyond. It is to symbolize the fact that our new ideals, our new world here, is completely transparent. It also signifies how open his mind was and how it should inspire other men to open their own minds to new ideas. It is especially glorious on a clear night, when his head looks to be full of stars."

Gordon could see what the father meant, but to Gordon it still looked like there was a giant hole where the man's head should be. "It's very large. How tall is it?"

The father said, "I'm glad you notice that. It is the tallest statue in any land. It is exactly thirteen feet taller than the statue in Thure."

Gordon realized it was a way to show off. He wondered if the thirteen foot difference was a coincidence, since the number thirteen was so important in his own kingdom. It reminded Gordon that he was only thirteen-years-old in a land about as far away from his home as a person could get. He had no idea if anyone knew where he was, or how he was going to get out. He decided to try to focus on what he could do, which was learn about these people. "What are those buildings over there?"

The father replied, "Why don't you explain that, Coltun. I see that I must go meet with a member of the outer council. It should just take a few moments."

Coltun was obviously not excited with his new task. "These buildings, young... young man are the seat of power in our land. The curved semi-circular buildings that you can see here are where many offices are, and where the outer council meets to decide on important matters. It is quite the honor to even be able to work in these buildings."

"Do you work there?" asked Gordon.

Coltun replied proudly, "Yes, I have the honor to work there. And on occasion I am sent to the buildings that you can just see in the center of the outer circle. Those are the Inner Circle chambers."

"I see. What happens there?" asked Gordon.

The man looked as though Gordon had just asked him what *air* was. "That is where the great father and his inner council meet."

Gordon didn't think Coltun understood his question. "Yes, I understand that. But what do they do there?"

The man looked incredulously at Gordon again, as if he were speaking a language that Coltun had never heard before. "That is where the inner Council meets. To decide *the most important matters.*"

Gordon felt that if he asked the question again he would get the same answer. He supposed that the man probably didn't know and maybe had never asked himself what happened there. "Oh, I see," was all Gordon said.

Looking around, Gordon noticed that the area seemed deserted. "Where are all the people? Is it a festival day?"

Coltun said, "Oh no. We have only three festival days a year. Work is very important to us. We had the areas you will see cleared of most people. The father is so loved, he would spend all day just shaking hands with people."

"He cleared all this, just for me?"

The father came back over to them. "Gordon, I'm sorry son, but there is an urgent matter that requires my attention. Coltun, you can finish the tour of the city for our young visitor here. I've already assigned two guards to come escort you, in case you need anything. We will talk again later, Gordon," and the father walked away, back towards the man he was meeting. Gordon understood clearly what the guards were really for, but Gordon had no plans to escape.

The assistant looked a little uncomfortable, but he decided that he would make the best of it. "Well, yes, shall we go?"

"Can I see the inner and outer circle buildings?" asked Gordon.

Once again the man looked at Gordon as if he was insane. "Absolutely not. No one is allowed in those buildings that does not work there. It is against the law to be within fifty feet of them," said the man nearly beside himself. "We ... we can explore the rest of the areas the father has chosen."

Gordon was led around to a series of buildings. He noticed many other statues. As he looked around, he could see that most of the buildings looked new. Several statues he recognized from old myths and stories. The strange thing was they all had the same face. They all looked like the face of TrTorrin, the father. He couldn't see how they had been altered. Talented craftsman must have done the work. *The people here probably didn't remember they had different faces before.*

The first place he was taken was the museum. There were large rooms with paintings, statues, old suits of armor, and weapons from all over the kingdoms. "We have one of the finest collections of antiques in any lands."

"Oh, I thought Thure had the biggest collection," said Gordon innocently.

"That is a filthy lie made up by the other kingdoms to make us look less great than we are. You really must be careful who you listen to, my boy."

Gordon didn't really care if it was the second biggest collection or not. He couldn't stop smiling. He had read a lot of history. Many of his books had pictures of past Dard warriors, old gods, and fantastic weapons. But now he was seeing these things for himself.

In the middle of the big rooms, he could actually touch things that he knew were thousands of years old. He felt like he was touching history.

"Most of these things seem to be from Dar.... I mean from the kingdom that is no longer here."

"That is true. No honest person doubts that we have the largest collection of such objects," replied Coltun stiffly.

Gordon said, "I'm confused. The father said that your land doesn't like to look back to its history," said Gordon.

The assistant seemed annoyed. "No, young man. What the father said was that there are only so many things you can learn from history. That is one of the reasons we do not let outsiders into our kingdom. What he says always seems to get twisted up when people try to quote him."

"Sorry," said Gordon, wondering why the man was so upset at the smallest questions.

"It's all right. I just get frustrated with what other kingdoms think of us. We are not bad people," explained Coltun. "We appreciate beauty, even old things just like everyone else. It's me that should be sorry. I am giving you a bad tour. This is not usually one of my duties. Um, boy... Gordon, are you alright?"

Gordon hadn't heard the last of what Coltun said. He reached into his large pocket for a sour cake. He ate all of one and said, "I'm fine. Just a little out of balance."

Coltun said, "Oh yes, your sweetblood illness. We don't have a lot of that here. Those types of things happen in your kingdom where people eat so much."

Gordon was feeling better, but was suddenly angry. "The sweet-blood does not happen because I eat too much. No one knows why it happens, some people just have it."

"Please, I mean no offense," said Coltun. "It's just that our new way of living has fixed a lot of the problems the older kingdoms have."

"You have no illness here?"

Coltun replied, "Of course we do. In Extatumm, we just live a healthier life. We all exercise every morning, for instance."

"There is no cure for my illness. Exercise can't fix it."

"I didn't mean that. I mean…"

Gordon interrupted. "Can we stop talking about this please?" Gordon didn't like the attention his illness sometimes received. What he really hated was all the mis-conceptions about the sweetblood.

"I think that would be best," Coltun said, relieved.

Gordon was taken to a class room next. The children looked like they were about seven years old. The teacher was teaching them about the history of Extatumm. Gordon was only there for a few moments, but the only thing he heard the teacher talk about was the father. Before they left, Gordon noticed the same three poems that were on his bedroom wall, were also on the walls at the school.

The assistant took them to a different part of the city. Gordon noticed that many of the buildings were large square buildings. One of the buildings had smoke coming out of it. "What are they making there?"

The assistant's face was very proud. "Oh, that is one of our most important places. It's where the workers are busy making parts for … well, just different parts. We are very proud of our workers."

"Can we go inside?" asked Gordon, truly interested. "Oh actually, I think I'd better eat soon…" said Gordon, beginning to feel a little lightheaded. He realized he ate a little too much sour cake. He couldn't remember the last time he was tested. He had to rely on how he felt, which was dangerous with his illness.

"Of course. Let's go get something to eat, then we will take you back to your guest quarters," said Coltun.

* * *

The father stared at the man calmly and looked him over one more time. "That is a very bold proposition. Why should Extatumm trust you? Why would I trust you?"

"You should always trust the man that has nothing to lose and no reason to lie," said Darion.

"There are always reasons to lie. And trust is never given, it must always be earned. How do you plan to earn my trust?" asked the father.

"I have only recently begun to learn how to speak plainly. So let me try with you. I want to be king. I want the queen out. I have only a few thousand men and she has an army and lots of ancient royal blood to hold alliances. We both have rights to the crown. Mine is stronger, but the people have chosen her. The people don't know what they want," said Darion, "I want to give them *me.*"

TrTorrin agreed. "The people must always be led to what is best for them. They will never go willingly. But how can I help with your problem? My land and its peoples keep to ourselves. We have not gotten involved with other kingdoms before."

"While that is true, the world is rapidly changing," said Darion. "If you were to help me become king, you would have a great ally in my old kingdom. An iron friendship that cannot be broken."

"Like any strong metal, iron can melt. If there was a way I can put you on the throne, there is no guarantee that you wouldn't simply ignore our friendship after you became king. The other kingdoms are not friendly to Extatumm. There would be much temptation for you to go against us."

"I have a few ideas about that," said Darion.

As Darion laid out his detailed plans, the father couldn't help but smile.

* * *

The assistant Coltun led Gordon to a large square building not too different from the factory they had just passed. There were two doors. The one on the right was on the second floor, at the top of a flight of stairs. The other door was on the left, on the first floor. It was open, with a long line of people standing outside, waiting to get in.

"What is this place?" asked Gordon.

"This is where we eat," replied the assistant as they headed straight for the second floor. The guards stayed outside as Gordon and Coltun went into a very large dining area. About half the tables were empty, but they still had to wait to be seated.

There were windows overlooking another room on the first floor. Gordon realized it must be the room with the line out the door. There were hundreds of people, and all the table appeared to be full. Gordon asked, "What was that line outside?"

"Those were the factory workers," said Coltun, joining Gordon by the windows overlooking the other room. "That is the workers' dining room."

"Oh. Why doesn't everyone eat together?" asked Gordon.

"We separate the people that work for the councils and the people that work in the factories, simply as a matter of schedules."

"Schedules?"

"You see, the workers all eat the same thing so that they can be fed very quickly and get back to the factories. This dining room here is for the council workers that have important work to do," Coltun indicated the other people in the room. "Didn't you notice that all the men in this room have beards?"

They were told their table was ready. On the way to their table, Gordon noticed that all the men in the room did indeed have beards.

A woman came up to their table and asked, "Would you like the beef or chicken today, councilor?"

Coltun replied, "We will take two beef please. Wine for myself and milk for the boy," replied the assistant. The girl rushed off and came back with the drinks quickly.

Gordon asked, "Why did you mention the beards?"

"Oh, don't you know? Only council workers that run the kingdom are allowed to grow beards, to honor our founder."

"Oh. I see. Sorry, but why doesn't everyone eat together again? I still don't quite understand," asked Gordon.

"You see, Gordon. The old system with the kings and queens, they got rich from other people's work. That has been done away with here. We are all equal and we work for each other. For instance, we all get served the same thing in this room every day, depending on what is available, so that our minds are strong to run Extatumm. The workers get food that makes them work hard, mostly vegetables, to keep them strong. And they all get the same amount of food, depending on how much they need, of course."

Gordon was still confused. "What do you mean, 'how much they need'?"

"Well, for instance, the women that work in the factories require a certain amounts of food each day. The men that work in the fields are usually much larger and require more food. You see, we all work as hard as we can and we all receive what we need. That way, nothing is wasted. There is a special committee that figures out how much each person needs. You should have seen how it was before. I was just a boy, but I remember. The kings and queens ate like pigs, while many people in the kingdom went hungry. We have done away with that. No one goes hungry in Extatumm now."

"No one is ever hungry?" Gordon asked, impressed.

Coltun said, "No. Well, except for a few problems we have in some of our distant villages. But we are working on that! When everything is properly in place, everyone will be equal, no one will go hungry, and no one will have to struggle for the daily necessities of life."

The men at the tables near them nodded in agreement with Coltun's explanation. He looked around again at the room full of bearded men. Many of them had glasses of wine. He wondered what they were given to drink in the lower worker's dining room. Gordon looked at the very thin serving girls, and realized that all the people serving food were female. Gordon thought this was strange, but didn't know how to ask Coltun about it.

Gordon said, "Sorry. I know I'm asking a lot of questions. It's just that I'm new here and I don't know how things work. I just … I'm still confused as to why there are two separate dining rooms."

The assistant went back into teaching mode. "Oh no. I want you to understand so that you'll know how much more modern and fair our way of doing things is. These men here in this room all have very important jobs running Extatumm. These men make sure animals are raised and farms are being planted. They make sure that the soldiers get trained. We are all very busy men and we can't wait in line all day to eat. If we don't do our jobs, if we don't organize the committees, if we don't make sure all the paperwork gets to the right people, then the workers down there would starve. Oh, pardon me a moment, Gordon, I have to go say hello to the leader of the building committee." He leaned over and whispered to Gordon. "It's always good to have friends in important places."

"Okay," said Gordon, trying to puzzle out why it all didn't quite make sense.

When Coltun returned, they finished their meal and went back down the stairs. Gordon ate all he could and felt in balance again. He wondered what his sweetblood number was, but only Loren knew how to test for that. He got sad thinking of Loren still in prison so far away. *I have no idea how to help anyone, not even myself.*

As they left the building, Gordon noticed that there was still a long line leading into the worker's dining room. He wondered how long it would take to get them all fed. Gordon couldn't help but notice that the dining room he had just come from was nearly half empty. He also wondered exactly what the workers ate. Somehow he didn't think it was as good as what he had just eaten.

They walked back to the founder's statue to see if the father was finished with his business. TrTorrin was standing outside of the building talking to some men. As they got closer, he thought one of the men looked familiar. But he couldn't quite place where he had seen him.

The father walked to them and said very cheerfully, "How was your tour?"

"It was very interesting, thank you. I think I've learned a lot," said Gordon. Coltun looked very pleased with himself.

The father nodded to the assistant and said, "You've done well, Coltun. I'll take Gordon back." Coltun went to the men waiting and TrTorrin led Gordon back to his room. "So son, what did you see today?" the father seemed genuinely interested, although Gordon sensed that he was also in deep in thought about something else.

"Well, I saw a lot of workers. We ate in the upper dining room, and then your assistant told me about how your kingd … how your lands work," Gordon said a little uncertainly. "There's just a few things I don't understand. He said that everyone is equal, but…"

"Go ahead and ask any question. I'll be happy to answer."

"It's just that… If you are all equal, then how are you their leader, their 'father'?"

The father smiled. "That does seem contradictory, doesn't it? Why would we overthrow a king and queen and then install a leader? Well, there are two answers. The kings and queens ruled because they thought the gods said they should. They had the power, and they felt they owned all the land. They could tell the people to do whatever they wanted. In Extatumm, everyone has an equal voice in how things are done. And we won't always have a Leader. Extatumm won't always need a guiding father."

"But you have one now, why wouldn't you have one later?" asked Gordon.

"You have to understand that we overthrew the king and queen not that many years ago. So it has been a lot of work just getting everything to work. The people weren't used to having freedom. So I have a responsibility to the people to fill the role as father. We are still transforming from one system to the other. Believe me, Gordon, I thought this process would be done long ago, but the people aren't quite ready yet. Hopefully, in another five years or so, they will be."

"But, don't you trust your own people to make the right decisions?" asked Gordon.

The father laughed and said, "You know, if I believed in kings or gods, I might be able to see why they would have put a smart boy like you in that role. And yes, of course I believe people will eventually make the right decision. But they must be guided until they are fully capable of thinking the right way. I think of myself more as their father than their leader because I'm not in charge of them, I'm simply here to guide them. We have to have committees of smart people to make sure everything gets done the right way. It's a very important task we leaders have."

A lot of what the father said sounded logical. Gordon could understand everything that he was saying, but there were things that just didn't feel right. He couldn't put it into words.

As they passed the statue, he looked through the void where the man's head should be. He remembered what Coltun had said about certain people being allowed in those buildings. Gordon looked back at the statue. "What happened to the founder?"

This was a question the father didn't seem ready for. He seemed to be feeling many things at the same time. Finally, he replied, "The saddest day in my life was when I found out that the founder was just as flawed as any other man. He was discovered doing things … that he wasn't supposed to. Bad things. I didn't want a few terrible acts to undermine all the good we had done together. So I separated him from the public. I quietly put him in prison to protect him from himself. He was like my brother. He was found dead the next day. No one knows how he died, but we suspect he couldn't live with the things he'd done."

The father's voice and so full of emotion, he seemed genuinely affected by the memory. Gordon looked at the father, expecting to see tears in his eyes. But there were none.

"There are very few people that I've told that story to, Gordon. I hope you will respect that, and not repeat it. I did what I had to do for Extatumm."

TrTorrin and Gordon walked back to his chamber where the guards were once again posted outside his door. He tried to imagine what terrible things Ollander Adair might have done or how he mysteriously died in prison. As Gordon walked around his room, he thought of what he had learned and, once again, studied the poems on the wall. He would continue trying to puzzle out Extatumm.

Chapter 9

Merry Meetings

As they neared the forest, queen Ellice could not believe how big it was. The tops of the trees looked like a giant blanket of leaves over a vast green bed. They were flying in from the canyon side, where the forest abruptly rose from the rocky cliff wall. As they came lower, and more level with the trees, Ellice realized how tall they really were. They were easily as tall as the statue in Thure. Some of the trees she could see must have been as large around as an airship.

One of the trees was moving. At first Ellice thought it was falling towards them. She quickly realized that a part of the tree was being slowly lowered. As it was lowered, she saw that it was actually a platform with large heavy ropes on either side, a bridge for the airship to attach to. One side had been left to look like the tree trunk, and the other was a flat surface for them to walk off the airship and into the fortress.

The airship floated, docked, and was tethered to the tree bridge. Mantuan and the others went into the forest. The queen planned to stay on board until all of the delicate papers were unloaded. Mantuan came back smiling and said, "Leave them on board. I will see they are handled safely. You need to come with me, my queen."

The queen was weary from the long travel. Hopefully Mantuan was going to show her a bed where she could rest. He led her into a room where a few people stood talking. Before Mantuan could lead her to the group, she recognized a voice. "Loren?"

The man stopped talking and slowly turned around. Without saying a word, he rushed to her and hugged her tightly. She hugged back, and through his tears he said, "I don't understand ... Ellice, I don't understand ..."

Her tears flowed freely as she replied, "Everything will be okay. Everything is all right now."

Loren replied, "No it's not, not yet. I was just told that Gordon was taken. I tried to protect him, Ellice. I tried so hard all these years."

"No, Loren. None of that. You were the one that saved my boy and raised him. Forgive me, Loren, I had no idea you were alive or I would've found my way back to you both."

"We are all lucky to be alive. How are you here? Oh sorry, Ellice, this is Denogg of the family Xoss."

Ellice put out her hand. "You're Santovan's brother. He has been a great friend to me."

Denogg began by taking the queen's hand but couldn't help himself. He hugged her instead, much to her surprise. "My queen, it is a good day."

Loren replied, "It is. I have so many questions, Ellice. I can't believe you are really here. I wish we could enjoy it more, but now I have to focus on getting Gordon back. Where did Mantuan go?"

Queen Ellice, Loren, and Denogg went to find Mantuan, who had quietly gone off to let them enjoy their reunion. Mantuan was receiving reports from the men and women who lived in the fortress. He was talking gravely with several of them when Loren approached.

They were still speaking when Loren interrupted. "Mantuan. We have to talk, right now."

Mantuan, avoiding eye contact with Loren, said, "We'll talk later, Loren. I have some things to attend to now."

"We will speak now!" Loren shouted and quieted the entire area. Queen Ellice did not know what to make of this. Denogg just stood there, looking uncomfortable.

No one knew what to expect. The old Mantuan would have turned around and knocked Loren flat. Instead, Mantuan turned to Loren gently and said, "I know why you're angry. We've all gone through a lot and there is still much to do. Go enjoy your sister. I will come to you soon, and we can all sit down and talk then. Agreed?"

Loren wanted to demand answers now. He wanted to stay angry, but Mantuan was right. Ellice was alive. He agreed with a nod and went off to talk with his sister about all the lost years. Mantuan was true to his word, and soon came to them with food and drink. He said, "Try the berries, they're delicious. We grow them right here in the trees."

The five of them: Mantuan, Loren, Denogg, Queen Ellice, and Aline all sat down in relative comfort for the first time in recent memory. They shared their versions of everything that had happened. Denogg was almost speechless to hear the tales. "I should have moved out of the old kingdom years ago. This all sounds very exciting, *much* better than being in prison. How is my brother, by the way?"

"He looks very well, a little thinner than you. Although you look like you lost a few pounds rotting in that cell," said Aline.

"Never one for tact, are you, my girl?" asked Denny.

They all laughed.

Queen Ellice shook her head, "I never thought I'd laugh again. I never thought I would rejoin the world, or would have any reason to feel happy."

"And I figured I was a dead man. Either by Trunculin or by the queen of Thure. I was glad Gordon got away from Thure. I was devastated when I heard he died. Now he's alive, and so is my sister, but we are still not all together." Loren's tone change as he turned, "Mantuan, why did you involve Gordon?"

Mantuan took a moment to respond. "I knew how angry you would be with me, Loren. I saw no other way than to have Gordon be chosen king. It was one more way to put pressure on Trunculin, and make sure he was undone from every angle. If we could fake a choosing, we could show that Trunculin did too."

The queen said, "But the danger was too real. You were not there to protect him personally. Loren was no longer at the palace. It was too risky, Mantuan."

"I was always able to protect him indirectly. I was in contact with Aline. Many others are helping us from within the palace. No one imagined that Gordon would have that vision and collapse. It allowed Trunculin to close his grasp around Gordon quickly."

"And what does this vision mean?" asked the queen. "No one in my family, or Daymer's family, was ever any kind of mystic."

Mantuan shook his head. "No one knows what it means. I'm only guessing, but I think that Trunculin may have employed a mystic to try to control Gordon's mind. Since the guild is so closed to outside influence, no one can prove it. I do have someone working on that. Maybe Gordon has some small gift for seeing the future, and when Trunculin's mystic was in his mind at the crowning ceremony, it may have triggered something like a true vision, like an echo in a canyon, amplifying what is already there. Maybe Gordon has talents that no one knows about."

Loren said, "Gordon described a world on fire. I wouldn't be surprised if Trunculin is trying to make alliances, ones that lead to war. Our world hasn't seen war on that scale before."

Mantuan said, "And I just had a disturbing report about airships."

Everyone got nervous. Ellice asked, "Are Brenddel's airships on their way here?"

Mantuan shook his head. "No. No, I have defenses built for that. It's much stranger news. The reports say that my agents have seen airships near the outlands. The problem is that the airships that they spotted are clearly not anything we have seen before. They say they are huge, and that they almost appear to be made of metal. We believed Extatumm might be building them, but not on this scale. That can only mean war."

"Extatumm hates Artoth and they are closest to them. The two kings have weakened their own kingdom with their fighting. They wouldn't expect an attack by air from Extatumm." offered Aline.

Queen Ellice said, "It could be for a simpler reason than that. Trunculin has always wanted total control. I have read the first thirteen's law book and I know what our kingdom was meant to be. It called for people to be free to make their own decisions. It was about kings being chosen at random, so that there was less corruption. The people in control of their own fate. When I was secretly gathering information in Extatumm, everyone talked of equality, while their leader had total control. Maybe Trunculin sees an ally in this 'father's' total control of his people."

"What are you saying? You think the firstcouncilor shared the airship plans so that he and TrTorrin could eventually dominate all of the kingdoms?" asked Denogg.

Mantuan replied, "Maybe split the world in half and rule it?"

Loren commented, "That is hard to believe. But if that is even partially true, all the kingdoms would have to fight, and every kingdom would be in danger."

Aline nodded. "A world on fire."

Chapter 10

Angry Return

After days of seas that were never calm, Brenddel and his men finally made it back to the kingdom of the thirteen.

When they left Artoth, outside the gates of the canal they had buried their dead at sea. They came home now to a dark bay. Brenddel had sent word to Trunculin of all that happened, or at least most of it, in letters with faster merchant ships. The reports should have arrived at least a day before they did; yet, no one was here to meet them.

Brenddel had asked for enough coin so that the watership they hired could be paid. He left the men on the boat and went to the bay master, inquiring if anything had been left for him. There was a secured box with enough coin to pay the ship's pilot. There was a little extra for the pilot and his men to stay overnight. That way they could enjoy the diversions near the docks before heading straight back to their lands.

Brenddel and his men slowly made their way back to the palace. He told his men to take double rations and enjoy the next day off to rest up from their journeys. Brenddel headed straight for the firstcouncilor. Even though he expected to be met at the dock, at least the firstcouncilor had left enough coin for him. Brenddel was sure Trunculin was trying to make a point by not meeting him and was not looking forward to their conversation.

He arrived at the firstcouncilor's chamber. Trunculin didn't look up at first. He was furiously looking over papers while drinking a glass of wine, or maybe something stronger.

Brenddel said, "Firstcouncilor, I have returned to give you my report in person. If you are busy, I will say good night to the king and come back when you are ready."

"Don't bother the king. He's already asleep. Will you have a drink with me? I had a few drinks in honor of your letter. Quite the tale. You found Mantuan and Gordon alive, but you lost them, and an airship."

"Are you sure you still want to offer me that drink?"

"Yes, yes. Sit. Even though I'm not pleased, the least I can do is offer a drink."

Brenddel poured himself a drink and realized it was definitely something stronger than wine, which was just fine with him. "I have a plan for finding Gordon and Mantuan. We have some other things to discuss that I did not put in the letter."

"Is that possible?" Trunculin picked up the letter and read it. "Let's see. My agent Arasta fell off the airship, and you were attacked by two of the fin creatures. You paid an outrageous sum to get into Artoth, where you did not find the murderers, but did find Mantuan and Gordon, both alive. The boy was then mysteriously taken. Mantuan's men stole your airship and the rest of my coin." He continued reading. "And then the two kings killed four of our men. Are you telling me there's more than that?"

Brenddel knew that he deserved all of that. The mission had gone wrong in every way possible. *That seems to be happening lately.* Brenddel was not used to failing.

"What I didn't put in the letter was that Darion and I both went in the councilor's stead to help negotiate. The only problem was that we didn't know what we were negotiating. Imagine how surprised I was to find out that someone in this kingdom sold plans for the airships. We even furnished gas to get them started on their fleet, so I was told. Apparently, we are also planning some sort of alliance with Extatumm."

Trunculin took another swallow and studied Brenddel closely. "There are many fronts a kingdom must fight on, outside of the actual battlefield. I had no idea that the leader of Extatumm would contact me. He wanted to talk about a possible alliance, only months before choosing a new king. I had to send Arasta secretly to see if it was even possible. And why are you so quick to think that I was the one to sell the plans for the airships? It was obviously the slaver king. He was getting slaves from them. Doesn't it make more sense that he was the one that sold the plans? You know that he was lining his pockets with coin from the kingdom. There was no end to the king and queen's evil deeds."

"The man I spoke with said that you were the one who sold the plans," said Brenddel, taking a drink.

"What possible reason could I have? This offer for a meeting between our kingdom and their leader came out of nowhere. I had no contact with them before that. Why would you believe a perfect stranger over me? You and I keep many mutual secrets. I wouldn't want to upset any of our arrangements," Trunculin said, taking another swallow.

Brenddel said nothing, thinking over what Trunculin had just said. It did make sense that the slaver king would stop at nothing to line his own pockets. He decided he would have to believe Trunculin, until he proved otherwise.

"Fair enough," said Brenddel. "I also believe the murderers were from Extatumm. It's just a gut feeling, but when I said I had to look for the murderers in Artoth, the Extatumm contact reacted very strangely. I was busy with Mantuan. Darion went with him to see what he could find out."

Trunculin leaned back in his chair and took a long swallow. "That may not have been the best thing. There's no way to know what Darion really hopes to gain. He may have gone there under the guise of helping us, while secretly securing an alliance for himself. I don't trust him… but we shall see. Oh, I also have some news. The queen released Loren and Denogg."

Brenddel nearly choked on his drink. "What? Why did she do that?"

Trunculin knew he couldn't tell Brenddel everything that had happened. "I have no idea. I suspect her grandmother gave her bad advice. But whatever the reason, they escaped by watership. We have no idea where they may have gone. Do you?"

Brenddel was angry again and poured himself another drink. "I'm guessing he has found a way to meet up with Mantuan. Do you know who would have taken Gordon?"

"My first thought would have been the treacherous Thurian queen. But that would make no sense, since she became convinced that neither Gordon, Loren nor Denogg was involved in the plot after all. She herself may have had the king poisoned. Maybe it was Darion. Whoever the murderers were, it doesn't matter now. No one is being held for the crime. Our alliance with the queen is publicly intact, but privately in tatters."

"So, who took Gordon?" asked Brenddel again.

"I have no idea. I have agents out sniffing around. One thing is certain, though, you don't take someone unless you're looking for ransom."

"Or you are looking for a slave," added Brenddel darkly, finishing his drink.

"In one case, the people that took him will contact us for ransom. In the other, we have nothing to worry about," said the firstcouncilor taking a drink. "I know you need to rest. After that, we need to prepare a diplomatic airship to escort the father of Extatumm here to meet our king."

Brenddel asked, "Why can't they use one of their own airships?"

"They're not yet ready to let the world know that they have built their own," said Trunculin.

"What are we getting out of it? It seems like we're giving, and they're taking."

"You haven't seen all of the reports that the councils have been studying. Our gas fields are slowly running out of gas. And as it turns out, they have discovered a way to make gas in a distant part of their own land. We must look towards the future." The gas shortage was a lie, but Brenddel wouldn't know that.

"How long have you known this?"

"For a year now. We have sent out teams to try to find a new place to mine gas in our own lands, but so far, nothing."

"I don't like the idea of being beholden to another people. Our kingdom has always been independent. We still don't know if they'll prove to be our enemy or not."

"This is the first step. We must meet in good faith with their leader and see what we can do. How soon can you get a transport together?"

"After I sleep for a full day, I can have it done within the week. We can't go back through the canal, though. I will have to take a mountain pass around Artoth."

"Good. I will send word tomorrow. Did your watership from Artoth stay overnight?"

"Yes," said Brenddel, "but they will be in no condition to leave tomorrow. They are enjoying all that the port has to offer."

"I'll send a message with another fast watership then," said Trunculin as both men finished their drinks. Brenddel departed for much needed rest.

Chapter 11

Father and Son

"Is that from Trunculin?" asked the father to his assistant.

"Yes, Father. We just got a message that they are ready for the meeting. They will be sending their ship soon. Your response?" asked Coltun.

The father smiled and asked, "Has Darion already left to speak with the queen?"

Coltun replied, "Yes. He left yesterday with one of our councilors, a member of the inner circle. Do you really think it will go well?"

"I doubt it. But it doesn't matter. If she is intimidated and agrees to Darion as king, then we have won the battle with no blood spilt. If she imprisons or kills him, we will have an excuse to attack. Either way it doesn't change our time line. Our plans are still intact."

"When will the inner council inform the outer council of our plans?"

"There's no need to worry about that. The outer council will go along with anything I say. No more challenges, they are as ready for war as I am. Contact Trunculin and tell him we would be honored to receive his airship. Tell him we have a special gift for him, but don't tell him what it is."

"You mean, the boy? You're taking Gordon with you?"

"Yes. I had thought the boy might be useful to keep here in case negotiations went badly. But I think a better tool will be to return Gordon to the firstcouncilor. Then, their kingdom will be busy putting him on trial and executing him. That distraction will be the time we need for our next step."

"Brilliant, father."

"Now all I have to decide is, do I tell the boy ahead of time? Or surprise him when he sees the airship coming? I think I will go pay our guest a visit."

The father walked down to Gordon's chamber, past the guards, and knocked on the door. "Come in," said Gordon.

"I hope I'm not disturbing you," said the father, entering the room.

"I was just reading the book you gave me, the collected writings of the great thinker Ollander Adair. It's kind of interesting." Gordon placed the book down.

The father sat in the chair next to the bed. "Would you like to discuss it? Do you have any questions?"

"It says your kingdom controls all the factories and all the farms, right?"

"That's right. And we own all the buildings and all of the land. Why do you ask?"

"It's just that, well, my uncle owns his house where we live. In my kingdom, before all of this happened…"

"Do you miss it? Not being a king, not being someone important?"

"I don't miss that. I miss home, though." Gordon continued, "In the summer, we tend a little garden we have next to the house. We grow vegetables and fruit, and it was fun. My uncle let me have a little section where I would grow sweet potatoes, my favorite. He would grow herbs and spices for healing. And we would fix the roof together every summer."

"Sounds wonderful."

"It was. But I was thinking that if he didn't own the house, he would have to ask permission to plant his garden. I'm not so sure that he would have taken care of the house in the same way if he didn't own it; if it wasn't *his*."

"How very little you think of your uncle, my son. Of course he would repair the roof whether he owned the house or not. He wouldn't want the rain to drip on your face. If the house was here, we would have qualified repairmen come fix your roof to the standards of the committee in charge of building, but it would be fixed all the same. True, we would not let you grow a garden. But that's because we have a larger plan to grow big crops to feed all of the people, not just you and your uncle. We think of everyone in our land as our children. We must take care of them."

"I guess the question I'm really asking is, what are people working for? My uncle worked so he could buy food, clothes, and so that we could do fun things together. He was proud to take care of the things we owned. What do your people work for?"

"That's the wonderful thing. We work for each other. We work for the good of the whole, all of us, so that none of us are left behind. Come with me son. I want to show you something."

The father escorted him outside. Gordon inquired, "I hate to ask, but when I got here, I didn't notice it at first, but it seems to be getting worse every day. What is that smell in the air?"

"Of course you smell it. We all smell it. It is the waste system and it's a big mess. You see, there are three committees. Each one is in charge of a different part of how we get rid of our waste." He counted off with his fingers. "One committee is in charge of liquid waste. They are called the committee for efficient removal of all waste liquids, or CER-AWL. Another committee is the solid waste management service of the outer committee counsel, or SWMSOCC. They are in charge of everything *but* liquid waste. The third committee is supposed to coordinate the two committees so that everything gets done. One committee is still working on a report to fix the problem. The second committee has been trying to talk with workers who all believe they deserve double rations for that kind of work. The third committee hates the men on the first committee, and a nephew of an important committee member is in charge of the other committee. We have three more meetings to hold later this week," The father said, smiling, "If they don't fix it by then, I'll send them all to the gas fields."

Gordon felt a chill go up his back. The father led him to a factory. "This is where we process our grain for making bread and flour. Do you see that man there?"

Gordon saw men everywhere. The one he was pointing to was a very large man who was loading large bags onto an enormous cart drawn by horses. "That man there is named Savil. You see how strong he is and how much he can lift? Those bags weigh as much as some men. You see the other men loading the bags, but not as fast. Why?"

"Because Savil is stronger than the other men," guessed Gordon.

"That is true. But why doesn't he work a little slower? He doesn't have to walk as fast. It's because he is doing his very best all of the time. He doesn't get more food than the other men. He doesn't have a nicer house. He does it because he believes in what we are doing here. He knows that all of us will benefit if he works to the best of his ability. That is enough reason for him."

It made sense, in a way. Why else would the man work so hard if he didn't get anything more than the other men got? He looked around very carefully, and he noticed that the few men that actually noticed the father, started to move a little faster.

Gordon spotted a group of men to the left, behind a stack of boxes. They were just standing there talking. Two of them were sitting. He froze. One of them looked exactly like Denogg's servant. But before he could be sure, the man disappeared behind a wall. *Why would TrTorrin want the king of Thure poisoned?* Gordon thought.

He did not ask him about it.

Then he noticed something else. No one was smiling. Not the big man with the heavy bags of grain, and not the men talking. Then he thought back to the workers in line to get food. None of them where smiling, either. The only person that ever smiled in Extatumm was the father.

"You asked before, what are they working for? Here, we have no people that selfishly own a bigger house than his neighbor's. We all work for the good of all. And everyone gets what they need. In the other kingdoms, people beg in the streets for crumbs that the rich choose to give them. Here, everyone gets the same slice of pie."

That reminded Gordon of the upstairs dining room he had been to. Many of the men in those rooms were fat. He wondered how that was possible if everyone got the same slice of pie. Maybe some people got extra slices when no one was looking? He did not share these thoughts with the father as they walked back to his room. Instead he said, "I don't mean to be rude. You have treated me with kindness, and you have called me your guest. But we both know that's not what I am. What are you going to do with me?"

The father laughed loudly and said, "There's that bluntness again that I have come to admire. You *are* my guest and you have been a most gracious one, considering all you have been through. Actually that's what I came to tell you. I am sending you home son."

"Home? Really… When? How?"

The father laughed again. "You see, I am not the monster that locked you in the tower after all, am I? An airship will be here soon. I will escort you personally back to your own kingdom. That is, if you still want to go."

"What do you mean?" Gordon asked, surprised by the question.

"You could stay here if you like. It's just an idea. I don't know what waits for you in your own kingdom. I have no sons, only daughters. I would love a son as bright as you are. I know you value your kingdom's way of doing things. But they are old. Extatumm has taken all the old ideas and made a better, more correct way to live. I hope you will join us."

Gordon walked in silence next to the father for a while, thinking. He didn't want to stay in this place, no matter how much he wanted a father. Still, Gordon knew that if he went back to his own kingdom, he would be put on trial, imprisoned, and probably killed.

Gordon finally replied, "Thank you, but no. I have to go home no matter what will happen. It's… it's just the right thing to do."

The father lost his smile. He said, "I see. I will let you know when we are ready to leave."

They had arrived back at his chamber and Gordon offered to return the book. The father smiled again. "You can keep the book. It's a gift."

The father left, and once again Gordon was alone. He was still a prisoner in his chamber. He wondered if he would ever be free again, wherever he went. He stared out of the window, thinking of the small garden halfway across the world.

Chapter 12

Darion and the Queen

A group of guards escorted the two men. The queen said, "Our lawful brother returns. And with a stranger to us."

Darion bowed a little, as did the other man. "My queen."

"You are dressed strangely, visitor. I wonder why you are here," said the queen pointedly.

"This is a councilor from Extatumm, my queen. My mission took some very strange turns." Darion looked around before he continued. "Will your grandmother be joining us?"

"No. My grandmother is … she's resting now," replied the queen. Darion seemed relieved.

"About your mission, lawful brother. I was surprised not to hear from you. No message, no letter of any sort. I had wondered if I should send someone to fetch you."

Darion smiled. "My queen, forgive me. I know how it must have seemed not hearing from me. But strange and rather delicate things were happening that I simply had to say to you in person. If any of my notes would've been intercepted, they might have been misunderstood."

"Did you find the murderers?" the queen asked.

"No. We could not find any evidence of them. Our contacts in Artoth led nowhere. But we did see Gordon in the streets of the kingdom of the gods. He was coming out of the house of Denogg's brother."

"Gordon is alive? Did you bring him back?"

"No, my queen, there were … complications."

"Another failure. Did you do anything while you were there, except bring back an enemy of my family?" the queen asked.

"Gordon was with Mantuan, who … well, who is also alive. Brenddel tried to fight Mantuan and get Gordon, but failed. I don't know what happened after that. I left for Extatumm."

"I see. I understand. Quite the adventure. Why did you bring this councilor back with you?" asked the queen, again staring at the man from Extatumm.

"Trunculin is planning a meeting in his own kingdom between King Asa and TrTorrin, the father of Extatumm. It will take place soon, and that may lead to an opportunity for us."

"You mean a meeting between the *firstcouncilor* and the father. The king is simply a face for the public. We all know he has no power. How does this help 'us'?" she stressed, while looking into Darion's eyes.

Darion took note and replied, "Since our kingdom has been publicly aligned with the boy's kingdom, it follows that we may want to meet with the father as well."

"The alliance was forged in public, but quickly dissolved in private when I let the two prisoners go."

Darion nearly screamed, "You did what? I mean … I'm sorry, my queen, I simply … why? I don't understand."

"In my grief, I wrongly accused Gordon. It was obvious the boy had nothing to do with it. I had my own private reasons for releasing the prisoners. There will never be an alliance between Thure and Trunculin. Not as long as I am queen."

Darion did not hide his anger. "So you, for your own selfish reasons, decided to break our new alliance with the most powerful kingdom? Just like that?"

"And once again you seem to forget who rules here," replied the queen.

"Then an alliance makes even more sense between our kingdom and Extatumm. We would be wise to consider it."

"There's that word again. *We* don't make decisions together. The queen does not rule with a 'we' or an 'us'. Unless you're planning to get down on one knee and ask for my hand, I suggest you remember who rules Thure."

"Forgive me, my queen," said Darion. "I didn't mean to presume. I just wanted to let you know that the world is changing quickly and our kingdom ... your kingdom has historically been slow to change. It would seem to me that Thure could be left behind."

"Pardon me, my queen. Will you grant me a moment to speak?" asked the councilor from Extatumm.

The queen looked at the man. "Even though it is not our custom, I will hear you. Speak."

"Our great father greatly respects history. He was once a teacher, in fact. He knows of the greatness of Thure. He wants to offer you the opportunity to be a large part of this new world. He wants to shine the light of what we are doing, the new way we have found of living," said the councilor reverently.

"You mean, a way of living without kings and queens. And those kingdoms that choose not to accept his generous light? Will this father offer them fire instead?" asked the queen.

Darion replied, "I don't think there is any threat being offered ..."

The Extatumm councilor said, "My queen, the father wants nothing but peace, I assure you. But your brother is right, the world is changing ..."

The queen interrupted. "I see. This kingdom is very old. And just like TrTorrin, I've always loved history. I remember reading about a king who lived some hundreds of years ago. His name was Jeduum. Even the name sounds fat, doesn't it? And he was the fattest king that ever ruled. But somehow, he had a beautiful young wife. Her name was queen Bryn. They say that kings from other lands would come just to see how beautiful she was. When I first read about them, I got this comical scene in my head of this jolly fat old king and his young beautiful wife he would chase after ..."

Both Darion and the councilor looked confused, but they didn't want to be rude, so they listened.

"... One day, he was receiving agents from another kingdom. Just as this messenger started to speak, he tripped over his words as he noticed how beautiful the queen was. Well of course, the king was too fat to fight the man. So he had the man's head cut off right there, before the man could say another word. He sent the head back to the other kingdom with a blindfold over its eyes. And that was just for glancing at his wife. And by the gods I would do the same to you. Guards, take them!"

The guards grabbed Darion and the councilor quickly. Before they could protest, the queen was walking towards them.

Darion shouted, "My queen, what are you ..."

"Quiet, traitor!" the queen said, but kept her attention on the Extatumm councilor. "You come here to my kingdom, look me in the eyes, and tell me I must be a part of your new world. You imply that if I don't ally with you, that I'm against you. I made my choice the moment you dared walk into my kingdom. Your father scum TrTorrin killed my grandfather and made my grandmother flee her own kingdom in nothing but rags. I should have them stretch your entrails all the way back to your kingdom, or whatever you call it now. But I don't want your evil blood spilled in my kingdom. You go to your father and tell him that he should remember his history. Thure has never been taken by force."

"You are making a terrible mistake, my queen, please listen," said Darion desperately.

"And I will give you a choice, traitorous brother. Death in the same public square where I buried your brother, or go back to that filthy place forever."

Darion couldn't believe what was happening. He couldn't find any words.

"Your silence makes your choice. Guards, put this scum back on their ship. Now." the guards took the men away, put them back on their ship, and they sailed back to Extatumm. Two Thurian escort ships made sure they made it all the way to the canal of Artoth, waiting there to make sure they got through.

Onboard, staring ahead to his new reality, Darion focused on justice, hoping his ultimate plan would work. One day soon he would return triumphantly to his own kingdom.

Chapter 13

Asa and Brenddel

Brenddel finished his meeting with Trunculin, all the details finalized. His men were nearly ready, with only a few supplies to load on the two airships for the escort mission. *There will be no mistakes this time*, Brenddel promised himself. He had sent out three other ships to scout for his stolen ship. No luck so far. After this mission, he vowed to himself that Mantuan would hang upside down from the ship he stole as meat for the fin creatures.

There was just one more thing to take care of.

"Good day, my king," said Brenddel as he walked into the king's chamber.

Asa exclaimed, "Brenddel! You're back. I'm glad to see you. You've been gone too long, but I forgive you. So, when will you start to train me? Oh yeah, I wanted to tell you..."

Brenddel sat next to the boy, but didn't look at him.

"You're leaving again, aren't you?" said the king, knowing it wasn't a question.

"Yes, my king. It is my duty to stay near you as much as possible, but when there is another leader visiting, I have to be in charge of security for the visit. I'm leaving soon to go pick up the leader of Extatumm. Besides, you don't need me around. It looks like you've doubled your guard," said Brenddel.

Asa looked around nervously and said, "I guess ..."

Brenddel sensed something strange. He looked at the four large men, and realized Trunculin has changed the king's personal guards in his absence. He stood up and spoke to them. "I have private business with the king. Leave us. All of you."

The guards looked at each other and one said, "The firstcouncilor has ordered us to stay by the king at all times."

Brenddel said nothing and walked to the man who had spoken. He stood only inches from the man and stared into his eyes. The guard met Brenddel's gaze at first, but soon broke it and started looking around.

Brenddel said, "No. Don't look anywhere else. Look directly in my eyes. I am going to ask a question and I don't want you to answer with your mouth. I want you to answer it with your feet. Who do you fear more, the firstcouncilor or me?"

The man swallowed hard and opened his mouth, but closed it as he realized what Brenddel had meant. He used his feet to leave the room. The other guards did the same. Brenddel and the king were alone.

Asa was looking down at the floor. "You shouldn't have done that. Trunculin will be mad ... " he looked up to Brenddel, "... he gets really mad."

Why am I letting this boy affect me? Thought Brenddel. He said, "I must tell you a secret."

Asa asked, "What secret?"

"Our Firstcouncilor Trunculin is an ass," said Brenddel.

Asa started to laugh but it quickly turned into crying. He recovered himself and said, "Does it have to be you that goes? Those guards do anything Trunculin tells them to."

"My king, the firstcouncilor is ... well, I know some of the bad things he's done. I recently found out he's done far worse things than even I imagined. There are probably even more horrible deeds he's done that we will never know about."

King Asa shifted in his seat and tried to be strong in front of Brenddel.

"I have men that are loyal only to me. They will be your guard from now on. The firstcouncilor will not be able to change that, even while

I'm gone. I should have done this sooner. I am sorry, my king. I did not know how much I would be away from you."

"Is … is there any way I can stop being king?" asked Asa.

"I'm sorry, my king. Once the crown is accepted, the only kings that have not completed their trials are the ones that have died or gone mad," said Brenddel.

Asa couldn't stop the tears now.

Brenddel put his arm around Asa's small shoulders, comforting him the best he could. "Fate does not choose kings that are not strong enough. I believe Trunculin is already on the way to his downfall. He has gone too far, and his bad deeds may soon come to haunt him. You must be strong for a little bit longer. It won't take long to pick up this TrTorrin and bring him back. Then there will be more feasting and training. Things will get better. We will eat chocolate together soon."

Asa straightened himself and nodded. "I'll be strong, like you are Brenddel. Thank you for the guards. That will help a lot. But hurry back. The chocolate sounds good," Asa managed a smiled.

Brenddel returned it. "I'll make sure those other idiots don't come near you again. When I get back, they will guard the sewage tunnels, or worse. Until then, only my best men will be your personal guard. Goodbye for now, my king."

As he left, Brenddel stopped. And for the first time, Brenddel bowed to him out of respect, not just because it was his duty.

Chapter 14

Gates of Dard

Darion's watership finally arrived back at Extatumm. The envoy didn't know what to say to Darion. The entire way back, Darion hadn't lost any of his anger over what had happened in Thure. When they got through the several layers of Extatumm security, Darion leapt onto the dock and went immediately to find the father.

TrTorrin agreed to see him right away. While pacing back and forth, Darion and the councilor relayed all that had happened. The father listened and watched Darion pace angrily. When they finished, TrTorrin said, "We still have options, Darion. The plan we discussed left room for this possibility. Calm yourself. Sit, and have some tea."

"I'm exiled from my own kingdom, and you want to sit down and have tea!" said Darion, incredulous.

The father got to his feet and slammed the palms of his hand down on the desk. "I want you to stop acting like a rich, spoiled child. Sit down!"

Darion had not seen TrTorrin so much as raise his voice. He sat and the father poured him some tea.

TrTorrin was calm again. "This changes nothing. I will leave soon for the meeting in the kingdom of the thirteen. That will leave time for you to make plans and get everything ready for the next step."

"You are right. I knew this might happen. I just hate that she has the power to do this to me."

"Use that rage," said the father as he leaned closer to Darion. "Focus it on the object of your hate. But put it in a box inside you, until you need it. And then you can open it at the right moment; when you have seized the kingdom and the queen is in shackles before you."

"Good advice," said Darion, as a slow smile came over his face. "What's is the next step?"

"I have assembled a team, including our best generals. From now on, you and my assistant Coltun will work directly with them to finalize the plans. Depending on how negotiations go for me in the kingdom of the thirteen, we will determine the timing of the larger plan. Stay focused."

A knock came at the door and it was the father's assistant Coltun. "I'm sorry to disturb you. But the airship should be here soon."

"Thank you. Assemble the team. I'm on the way,"

"Coltun, take Darion to the generals. Let's begin the glorious new future."

* * *

Brenddel was concerned.

He wasn't sure of all the implications of an alliance with Extatumm, but that's all he'd thought about on the journey. Since Dard fell, Extatumm had no major allies or trading partners. Extatumm relied on trade with lesser lands for the few things they needed, or could not produce themselves. An alliance with a major kingdom, like the kingdom of the thirteen, might change everything for Extatumm.

When they won their surprisingly quick war and overthrew the kingdom of Dard, the whole world was stunned. Then the news came that they had killed most of the royal family, including the king. All of the other kingdoms were outraged. It didn't help when papers were published outlining their ideas, including a world with no kings and no gods. Since taking over the large kingdom, very little else was known about them.

Waterships that strayed too close were attacked. No one was allowed in the new glorious Extatumm. It seems like anything they heard about the 'father' was negative. Only months after overthrowing the king and queen of Dard, TrTorrin had tried to take back a large island called Asgonan, located between Extatumm and Artoth. It was a strategic prize, and Artoth had fought fiercely, even accepting the assistance of the kingdom of the thirteen. Mantuan and a few thousand soldiers fought with Artoth and won the island back. That's when Mantuan had found Brenddel. Extatumm had kept mostly to itself since then.

Brenddel pondered all of these things on the way to Extatumm. He feared dealing with these people would give Extatumm a better standing in the world. But mostly, Brenddel hated politics. When he was first training to be a guard, he had no idea that he would have to be around so many councilors and people that filed papers all day. It made him uneasy and tired.

He didn't remember Mantuan having to deal with all of these kinds of issues when he was firstman. *But after all, he hid many dark secrets from me.* Brenddel tried to shake Mantuan from his mind and focus on the task at hand. He had to admit to himself that he was a little excited to see one of the major wonders in all the kingdoms.

Brenddel had always wanted to see the Gates of Dard. He had heard about them all of his life, but he was never taken to them as a child. He had seen drawings of them in old books of history. They were the entrance to the Kingdom of Dard, but they were also much more.

Since the entrance to the kingdom was between two steep mountains, they built the gates to the kingdom hundreds of feet high. They were made of solid metal, ranging from gold at the top, to lead at the bottom. Built at least five hundred years ago, each of the seven metals panels included beautiful sculpted scenes of gods and kings.

Most men only got to see the gates standing at the bottom, looking up. But Brenddel wanted to be the first man from his kingdom to see the gates from an airship, straight on. He had heard that sunrise was the best time to see the gates, when the sun reflected brightly off of all the metal panels. The gates were said to nearly glow. His airship and his other escort airship came around the last mountain before going in straight towards the gates. He played a game with himself to see from how far away he could spot the gates. He especially wanted to see the middle panel made of bronze that depicted the great king Steppen wrestling with seven serpents.

He saw the gates, and he could tell that they were indeed several different colors. But as they got closer, he wasn't quite sure what he was seeing. His eyes tried to focus on the detail, but even as they got very close, he could see none. It appeared that some of the levels had been covered over with large sheets of metal fastened onto the wall. Other sections were covered with wood.

The top two panels made of gold and silver were no longer there. They had been roughly removed and Brenddel could see the core of wood that the gates center was made of. Apparently the gates were not solid metal after all, but simply sheathed in it. As he looked for the middle panel, his heart sunk. It had also been chipped away and defaced so you could not tell what the picture was. It looked as though a child had decided they didn't like their drawing and roughly scribbled it out.

All Brenddel could see over the wall was the top half of a large statue. It appeared to be a man, but the top was strange and appeared to have no face. As they got within fifty feet of the wall, slender towers appeared before their eyes, extending upward from behind the gate. Atop each one was a platform with several men. Each one was manning a large arrow gun. They were all aimed at the two airships.

One of the guards from the spire tower shouted, "No outsiders permitted in Extatumm."

Brenddel shouted from his airship. "We are here to escort TrTorrin back to our kingdom of the thirteen. I am Brenddel, firstman of my kingdom."

The man who had spoken to Brenddel waved his arms to the other men and the arrow guns were all lowered. The guard said, "Welcome to Extatumm. Our orders say that only one ship may pass. Your other ship will have to wait here. Proceed straight into the capital. You will see a landing pad just outside of the outer circle."

Brenddel waved his thanks and began to fly over the wall. The spire-like towers were already lowering out of sight as he entered the kingdom. Brenddel thought it interesting that they would build such devices, specifically as weapons to take down airships. I might have to look into that idea, now that another land has airships too, he thought.

Brenddel could see a few airships in the distance. They were too far away to make out any detail. He thought it was strange there were not more. The few he saw hardly constituted a fleet.

He focused and thought he might see some of the famous old buildings of the Dard kingdom. He read about them when he was younger, but nearly all the buildings were square and appeared new. He only spotted two older buildings. *Apparently they do not care about history here.* He was worried that he would not recognize this 'outer circle.' Then he focused on the statue, which looked to be the center of their kingdom. *Or whatever they call it now*, he thought.

At the statue's feet was what looked like a large, staring eye. There were two long buildings, one that curved upward in nearly a half circle, and the other above it curving downward forming another half circle. In the center was a round building that made the center of the eye. The image of the staring eye made Brenddel uneasy.

Brenddel now saw the landing pad that the guard had mentioned. In fact, it was a large series of landing pads over a great part of the land, larger landing pads than any in his kingdom. *Maybe there is a fleet of ships after all.*

Off a little farther, he saw large rectangles that also looked like landing pads. As he got closer, they looked more like large sails that had been laid out on the ground. He couldn't imagine what they were.

He could see a group of people standing on the pad waiting for them to land. He noticed a ground crew waiting to take his airship's ropes, so there was no need for his men to rope down. After his airship landed and was secured, he walked out alone to meet them.

"I am Brenddel, firstman of the kingdom of the thirteen. King Asa offers you peace and has asked me to escort the father, TrTorrin back to our kingdom to meet with him. I see you wear no red cloak today."

The man smiled, "Nor you. I am the father's assistant, Coltun. It's good to see you again Brenddel. The father will be here in a moment. We have a delegation of twenty. Are there ample accommodations for ten?"

Brenddel was confused, "Yes, of course. All twenty will fit on my ships comfortably. As per your orders, we had to leave the other airship outside of your gates. We will have to land somewhere and divide your staff ..."

"There will be no need. Ten can go on your ship. The father and the rest will be riding on his own airship," said the assistant.

Brenddel scowled. "That was not my understanding." He noticed in the distance that men were rolling back one of the large sails on the ground, as though they were rolling up a carpet.

"I am sorry, it was a last moment change," said Coltun. "The father thought it best."

"I do not like surprises. This is a delicate matter for my kingdom." But Brenddel had his eyes on the sails. The material that looked like sails had been rolled away and an airship was lifting out of the ground. The shape was unmistakable as it rose, but it was the size that troubled Brenddel. *So that's how they have hidden them*, he thought, *underground*. The ship continued to rise and as it turned slightly, Brenddel realized its true size. *It must be twice as long as my airship.*

The assistant had stopped talking as well. Everyone's eyes were on the giant airship as it headed their way. It was much longer than Brenddel's ship, but also much different. It was silver and black, with what looked like a kind of skin around the floating section. It must have been a light material, but in the sunlight the new ship looked like it was clothed in metal. Brenddel noticed rope ladders on the side. He would definitely keep his eyes alert for how this massive airship worked.

The ship came to the next landing pad. It made Brenddel's airship look puny and inferior. Brenddel assumed that was the point. *What will Trunculin's reaction be?* He wondered.

Brenddel looked over at the approaching delegation. He was sure the man in the center was the father. He was taller than most of the men and had something about him that set him apart. Other men and women surrounded him. The father was talking to someone that Brenddel could not immediately see. The person must be short, because the guard in front blocked him. Brenddel thought briefly of the short councilor that went flying off of his airship.

They arrived at the airships, and the father came right up to Brenddel and embraced his hand like they were old friends. "You must be the fierce Brenddel. I am TrTorrin. Shall we go?"

Brenddel was surprised at the father's openness. As he looked over the rest of the delegation, his eyes stopped on whom TrTorrin had been talking to. The father said, "Oh yes. I hope the firstcouncilor will like my gift."

As they boarded the two airships, one of the last people to board said, "Hello, Brenddel."

Brenddel replied, "Hello, Gordon."

Chapter 15

Out of Prison

"How kind of you to let me out of prison, granddaughter."

"That doesn't mean that I forgive you for making alliances behind my back," replied the queen of Thure.

Her grandmother retorted, "There was no conspiracy. There are not many people my age, and certainly none that I can speak to as an equal. He may only be firstcouncilor, but he has as much knowledge as a king. Maybe more."

"So you thought it was all right to run to him and tell him everything I was doing?"

"My dear, everything I do is to protect you. In this case, I was trying to protect you from yourself. I wanted this alliance for you so badly. But I forgot my code and nearly betrayed my own blood. That will never happen again, my queen."

"I have my own reasons for releasing those prisoners. You should have respected that."

"Exactly. You had your own *personal* reasons for doing it. And in that moment, you were not keeping what's best for your kingdom in mind. Did your actions change anything for the better?"

The queen did not want to answer. "No. It seems to have made things worse. But I had to do something."

"There is nothing you can do to save that boy. He must be controlled."

The queen was appalled, "Do you mean that you know what Trunculin is doing to the boy king?"

"No, I don't know how he is controlling the boy, and I don't want to. But, my dear, what did you expect? When you have a ridiculous system where you choose little boys at random to run your kingdom, there is always going to be someone who has the real power."

"How can I just stand by, when the real power is a monster?"

"People that rule often have to make difficult decisions. Things that some people would call monstrous," explained the grandmother. "I'm sure I would not approve of the way he controls the boy, but I understand that he must. And your insistence on meddling directly in those affairs cost us a very strong ally. Especially with this new threat from Darion and those people."

"Perhaps you're right. I don't approve of what the firstcouncilor is doing, or how he's doing it. I wonder ... how can we repair the damage?"

"I could speak to the firstcouncilor, if you like. By the way, that was a bit clumsy, my dear. Making it sound as though this was my idea. You want me to try and talk to Trunculin. Isn't that why you let me out of prison?"

"Yes. It is one of the reasons. But I also thought of the past, and realized how much you have been there for me. You have always guided me through this maze of royalty and leadership. Although I still feel betrayed by what you did, my head is cooler now, and I can see more clearly how things must be."

"Good. It's a difficult lesson to learn. Much of what kings and queens must do, they have to do for practical reasons. We must live in the real world. We don't have the luxury of dreaming of how the world should be."

"What's happening with King Asa is not right. But, that poor boy is on his own. Maybe with a repaired alliance, I can find some way to help him later," said the queen sadly.

"Yes, it is too bad. But I'm more concerned about this business with the boy's kingdom and the filth who stole Dard from me. Maybe you should think bigger, my dear, and take the boy's kingdom from him. This may be a good time to show the true power of Thure."

"That's ridiculous. I have no soldiers, only guards. The army of Thure is old and fat, like the rest of my kingdom," the queen replied. "But I am worried about this strange business. Especially since my brother-in-law is on their side now. Darion only has a small army stationed in Aspora. But we don't know what the other monsters have been doing behind the gates of Dard. I fear that they have been living in the dark too long. Bad things grow in the dark."

The grandmother agreed. "But now they may be coming out into the light. They would never attack Thure directly. Darion is not stupid. He knows the natural defenses of our kingdom. No one can take Thure by force. Not from land or sea, fat army or not."

"If Asa's kingdom makes a firm alliance with the scum that took Dard, there will be a new battlefield, one that we have no soldiers to fight in, and one with their airships. They will wipe out the last great trade that Thure has, our shipbuilding, by making them pointless. Or they could subdue us from the sky directly."

"Then I should leave now and go speak to the firstcouncilor," said the grandmother. "If I can convince Trunculin that Thure has more to offer than that monster TrTorrin, then we may have a chance."

"Then go now, grandmother. I am counting on you to mend this mistake I made."

"Maybe there is a place in this world for an old fallen queen, after all," said the grandmother as she left to start her journey.

Chapter 16

The Real Prize

The three air ships flew in formation towards the kingdom of the thirteen. Brenddel's two airships looked almost silly next to the massive black and silver Extatumm ship. Brenddel knew that they would not be allowed over the Artoth canal again, especially with an unknown ship from Extatumm. Brenddel flew through the Gantroh mountain range on the way to Extatumm. They would have to serve again.

The mountain range was well south of the canal, but treacherous. Useless to waterships, with only a narrow stream flowing through, it reminded Brenddel of a snake, with its sharply curving path through the steep mountain range. It also narrowed at many points, making TrTorrin's large ship an issue. But Brenddel knew this was the only path for them to follow.

The father stood alone by the railing at the front of his large ship. He was looking forward to the world around him. Gordon no longer felt like a prisoner. Not exactly, he thought. He was free to go anywhere on the ship, but for some reason he kept feeling drawn to the father. He wandered over to where the father was and leaned on the railing. The father started speaking as though they were already in the middle of a conversation. "Isn't it beautiful son? The way it all fits together? Land and water and sky. And only a handful of men can see the world from up here. It has made the world smaller."

"Smaller?" asked Gordon.

"Airships have only been around for a short while. Before, it took more than twice as long to get from place to place in a watership. Even our maps were less accurate, because we couldn't see the land from this high up. The world's gotten smaller because we can talk to each other across great distances even faster. Getting a note to your kingdom had to go by watership, by land, sometimes by bird or dog. It takes forever. As soon as we show the world Extatumm airships, the world will shrink even more. Messages, trade. A faster, smaller world."

"I haven't known a world without airships. They've just always been there."

"Exactly. You said you love history. But history is written every day. For years, the other kingdoms thought about us as some crazy men with strange ideas. When you have a son, he will know a world where Extatumm was always equal to other kingdoms. Or perhaps even greater than other kingdoms. When the world sees our new way of thinking, maybe your son, or his son, will know a world where there are no kingdoms at all; just one big world."

"Who will lead the new world? You?"

The father only smiled. "No, Gordon. A counsel of the most intelligent men will lead the world. And they will be working for the good of all the people, for all of the world."

"So, it's like a larger version of your inner council. A few would be in charge of the many. Won't there always be someone like a father? I mean, you're the father, the leader of your land."

"True, for now. As I explained before, that is temporary. Once we fix all of the problems, I will step down and a committee of very smart men will be in charge of the people."

"So, this committee of equals will write the laws for everyone else? If a few are in charge of the people, how is everyone equal? That just seems to go against itself. It sounds like a committee of kings. Or a bunch of councilors in charge."

"Many of the problems that my land has had are because other kingdoms are fighting our ideas so fiercely. If they would just accept that our way of doing things is a newer, better way, then they would see that their old ways no longer work. We must let the old ways die and the new ways take hold. You see, the more they fight our new ideas, the more they force us to fight back. They will come to understand that our system is the natural conclusion of history. It's the next step for the world."

Gordon still felt there was something that he was missing, that he couldn't quite grasp it. "But then ... if your system is the natural way, the correct way we should all do things, wouldn't it have already happened on its own?"

The father winked. "Sometimes history needs a push in the correct direction."

One of the father's guards came over to him and said, "Great father, someone is following us."

TrTorrin went to the back of the ship. He was handed a long spyglass and was surprised to see one of his own, older and smaller airships coming at them fast.

The father looked through the long glass again. He seemed concerned. TrTorrin thought of his five ships that had gone missing. Brenddel's ship broke formation and came closer to the father's airship. Brenddel shouted from his deck. "Do you know anything about this?"

"No. This is not us," replied the father.

"I had a bad feeling we would be attacked. You continue on course and my other ship will be your guard. I'm going to engage the ship. Any problem with that?"

The father shouted back, "No. Take it down."

Brenddel did not like what sounded like an order from the father. He shrugged off the thought and commanded his men to engage. The air space was wide enough for all the airships, but was starting to taper just up ahead. It was going to be the trickiest part of the trip. Difficult for one airship, worse now that he was forced to escort an airship of a larger size. He hadn't bargained for that. Apparently someone else had, since this was the perfect place to attack.

Brenddel had all of his weapons at the ready for the fire and arrow guns. All of his men were equipped with small arrow guns as well. The airship looked similar to theirs, but was much smaller than the giant ship that the father was on. This must be the first type of airship they built before they developed different designs, Brenddel reasoned.

It was clearly no match for Brenddel's ship. Apparently, the attacking ship realized this too, and started to sink lower, almost as though they were trying to go under Brenddel's ship. Brenddel smiled. His most powerful weapon was fire.

He would be happy to burn them out of the sky.

The large Extatumm ship and the guard ship were just starting to enter the narrowest part of the mountains. There will several blind corners coming up that they would have to navigate carefully. The pilot of Brenddel's other ship adjusted for the speed as all other eyes were watching Brenddel's ship engage the enemy behind them.

The attacking ship was nearly directly under Brenddel's ship. He was just giving the order to light the fire, when the smaller airship quickly gained height and came up underneath them. Brenddel knew that it was too late to get out of the way. He watched as the ship grew larger beneath them and it smashed into their deck, throwing everyone off their feet. Several men fell off of his ship, tumbling to their deaths.

Because the shape of the ship was rounded underneath them, it pressed up against the deck and tilted it to one side. The deck was still firmly attached to Brenddel's ship, but at this angle it made doing anything difficult. Two more men fell out as Brenddel held onto the center ropes on the deck. He watched one of the councilors from Extatumm fall. *Trunculin isn't going to like that.* Brenddel had to save the rest of his men and get away from the other ship to make evasive moves.

* * *

The people on the other two ships watched in horror as the smaller ship floated up and smashed into Brenddel's ship. They saw several people fall off. Nearly all eyes were out the back of the ships, watching the fight unfold. The only men on board not watching the battle were the pilots, who were busy steering the ships through the narrow mountain range.

The other soldiers had all gone to their stations to man weapons. The large arrow guns were versatile weapons, able to pivot in many different directions. They were all pointed to the back of the ships in case the unknown ship headed their way and attacked. As they came around the curve, it was only the pilots that saw another airship floating directly in their way.

Both pilots shouted to their men, but it was too late to stop the first attack. Several large arrows flew from the new ship in front of them, striking their ship's deck and crew. They pierced the gas filled section of Brenddel's guard ship. It immediately started falling from the sky. TrTorrin ordered his men to face full front with their weapons. He expected a volley of large arrows to come his way from this new ship again.

The father was surprised instead to see small arrows take out three of his men. The pilot of TrTorrin's airship knew it was dangerous to go alongside an enemy ship where the weapons could tear into the side, but he had no choice. He jerked the ship to the right so that he wouldn't run head-on into the new enemy airship.

The pilot of TrTorrin's large ship was close enough now to realize that the airship they were facing was from the kingdom of the thirteen. The two ships were so close now that the large gas-filled ships almost touched each other. TrTorrin's last two men standing were shot with a volley of arrows from the mysterious new ship. The enemy airship gained height and the father saw men on ropes coming down. This enemies' men were coming aboard TrTorrin's ship.

The new ship was just above as men climbed down, attaching large metal hooks to the railing. He knew they could use the rope ladders attached to either side of his ship to get to the deck. The new ship and the Extatumm ship were hooked together, and TrTorrin had too many wounded to stop them.

* * *

Brenddel had managed to gain footing and steered his ship away from the attacker. His deck was once again level. He told his fireman to release a stream of flames. The oil ignited and a stream of fire went straight down towards the other airship.

The smaller ship easily maneuvered out of the way. It was no longer directly under them, but had dropped again and pulled away from Brenddel's ship.

One of his men pointed towards TrTorrin's large ship. For a moment he didn't understand why there was another airship directly in their path.

Then he realized it was his ship. Brenddel saw that the airship blocking their path was the ship stolen from him in Artoth. Then he saw his guard ship drop from the sky.

Mantuan was here.

The small ship rose again and came up beside Brenddel's ship. It immediately started firing small and large arrows. The large arrows missed their targets, but the small arrows cut two of his men down. One fireman fell and at least two more councilors from Extatumm were hit as well.

His last soldier fired his large arrow gun and grazed the attacking airship. He knew it wasn't a mortal wound for the ship, but he could tell that there was gas escaping. The attacking ship couldn't engage much longer. He knew the enemy realized it too. He was close enough now to see a few people on board.

A woman wrapped her hands around her own railing and stared at Brenddel. His blood went cold when he saw Sandrell staring at him from the deck of the attacking airship. She stepped back to the middle of her deck and the ship started slowly drifting away.

Brenddel wanted to follow and finish off Sandrell's ship, but he had a duty to perform now that his guard ship was lost. With his one soldier left, and a few councilors still not quite dead, he made his way to TrTorrin's ship.

To Mantuan.

* * *

TrTorrin's ship was firmly attached to the enemies' ship. Their small arrow fire had taken out nearly every guard on board except for the pilot, Gordon, and the father. There were no soldiers left on board to stop the attack as men slid down the ropes and used his own ladders to board the deck.

The father drew his longknife as the first enemy boarded his ship. They came on board and surrounded TrTorrin and Gordon. To TrTorrin's right was a fierce looking young woman. To his left were three more men, one with a patch over his eye. All had knives drawn.

"What do you want?" asked the father.

Mantuan spoke. "I want a great many things, TrTorrin, Father of Extatumm. I want peace among men, I want people everywhere to stop being oppressed by their masters. But right now, all I want is Gordon. Hello Gordon."

"Hello Mantuan. Hello Aline," replied Gordon, trying to go to Mantuan, but the father held his arm in front of Gordon.

"You'll have to go through me to get him," said the father, raising his longknife higher.

"I have no time to argue," said Mantuan as he started towards the father. TrTorrin was about to attack, but felt a knife in his side.

"Stop," said Gordon.

The father looked quickly back to Gordon, who had drawn his own shortknife. The father regretted giving his weapons back to the boy.

"It's over TrTorrin. I'm leaving."

Gordon kept his shortknife up as he joined Aline.

"This saddens me. I guess this is goodbye, son."

"You're not my father. You were just my prison guard."

The father did not hide his anger. He used his knife and tried a thrust at Mantuan. Knocking it away, he slashed and connected with TrTorrin's wrist. The father's longknife fell from his hand. Mantuan gave a small salute and began to leave the ship.

"Why not kill me?" asked TrTorrin, holding his wrist.

Mantuan smiled. "Oh no, Father of Extatumm, I have bigger plans than that." Mantuan glanced at Brenddel's approaching ship. "Tell Brenddel to bring my axe next time we meet."

They left the ship. Two men stayed behind until the rest were up the ropes. Then the two men followed, unhooking the ships.

Before Brenddel could get near them, Mantuan's ship was already flying away. Brenddel reached the father's ship and knew he had missed Mantuan again. He stared in rage as Mantuan floated away. He wanted to chase the ship, but he had to attend to the wounded and TrTorrin. He came alongside the father's ship and saw that many were dead or wounded on the deck. The father was holding his wrist and wrapping it in some cloth.

"Will you live?" shouted Brenddel to the father.

"I will. It wasn't me they wanted. Gordon was the real prize. Their leader was a man with a patch. The long dead Mantuan, I presume. He said something about an axe."

Brenddel clinched his teeth, the truth confirmed, and said, "Was that one of your ships that attacked me?"

"It was my ship, but not my men. Some of my ships have gone missing. We thought they'd gone down in the deep waters during tests flights. Apparently not. They were clearly working with the man with the patch."

Brenddel was silent as he thought about an alliance between Mantuan and Sandrell. It was too much to think about at the moment. "Is your pilot alive?"

"Barely."

"Then we'll have to transfer everyone to my ship and get out of here."

"No. the wounded can't be moved. I can fly the ship. Just lead the way. The faster we get to your kingdom, the faster you can take your fleet and find them," said the father. "Why would they risk everything for the boy? He's been disgraced. He's not important."

"I don't know. But as soon as we get to safety, I'm going to find out. I will burn down the world to find them," said Brenddel firmly.

The father looked at Brenddel and believed him. Brenddel led the way and the two airships continued on to the kingdom of the thirteen.

Chapter 17

Deliver the Dead

"Are you sure you are ready, my king?" asked Trunculin, standing behind him.

"Yes. I'm sure." Asa shuffled his feet and looked over the papers again. He wore shoes for the occasion. This was his first speech, and he wanted to get it right. But the speech that Trunculin had written for him didn't make any sense. Why does Trunculin want to make an alliance with Extatumm, the people that openly hate kings? He knew he would get no answer if he asked, so he didn't.

Trunculin gently put his hand on Asa's shoulder and said, "You will do well, my king."

His touch almost made Asa pull away, but inwardly he smiled. The firstcouncilor had been furious when he found out the king had new guards, men handpicked by Brenddel. He had been angry, but he wasn't able to do anything about it. No one had hurt him since Brenddel left. He felt safer, still wishing Brenddel was here. But he wasn't, so the king slowly made his way out onto the balcony.

There was a great crowd awaiting him, and there was much yelling and applause. Asa's pulse quickened as he headed onto the balcony, grasping his papers firmly. He just knew that any second the wind would take them away. Luckily the wind was calm, and the young king tried to be as well. He stepped in front of the voice amplifier and began to speak the firstcouncilor's words.

"Thank you all for coming today. It feels good be back home. I ..."
The crowds roared their approval.

Trunculin had warned him about pausing for cheers and had even made red marks where he thought the cheers would come. There was a lot to remember, but he continued. "I wanted to assure you that I have returned from the great Kingdom of Thure with a firm alliance. The state of friendship in both of our kingdoms has never been better."

There were cheers again, but he heard a few shouts as well, shouts that did not sound good. But the overwhelming good cheers drowned these out. He continued. "And I have an announcement, a new way forward for our kingdom. Since I have been king this short while, we have been approached by agents of the distant land Extatumm."

There were definitely a lot of negative sounds, some boos and shouts. Asa thought that they might be split evenly down the middle, but there was really no way to tell.

Asa was sure this would happen, but the firstcouncilor just told him to read on. "I know this may sound strange, since Extatumm has expressed such dislike for kings and our way of life. Since I'm a new king, I spoke to many councilors about this and what advice they would give. Many of them said it was a bad idea..."

The crowds agreed with the statement, but Asa read on. "And as your new king, it seems logical that I would take their advice. But, with youth comes hope. I have hope that we can finally put any differences to rest."

Again, there was mixed results from the crowd, but Asa sensed that the crowd might go either way. "The father wanted me to travel to his land, or to a neutral kingdom to meet." Trunculin had written to sound forceful here. "But I said no!" Asa had practiced in his room for an hour the night before.

At this, the crowds cheered together, and Asa smiled to himself. *It's almost like I'm really connecting with the people.* "I told him the only way I would consider meeting is if he came all the way here to speak with me."

The crowd still seemed to approve, "I ordered my Firstman Brenddel to take the airships and bring the father of Extatumm here to talk. In this peaceful meeting, the first one of its kind ever between our two peoples, I will secure a peace that will last for all time. Any bad blood between us will be settled right here!"

There was a mixed response again, but Asa felt that it was still mostly positive. He faced the crowd. Even though the speech was done, he felt like he had convinced most of them. He didn't know what else to do. Without thinking, he raised his fist in the air. He wasn't sure why he did it and hadn't practiced it the night before. He just felt the sudden urge to gesture to the crowd so they knew the speech was over. For the first time, he felt like a king.

Asa understood that he wasn't really in charge of anything. But for that one moment in front of the cheering crowds, he felt that everything might be okay. It felt like the cheers lasted all day.

Only Trunculin coming up behind him broke the moment. He put his hand over Asa's balled fist, raising it a little higher and then using his other arm to point to the king as though he were introducing a great performer. And it worked. The crowd roared even louder. Both Asa and Trunculin smiled to the crowds.

Through his smile, Trunculin said, "You did well, my king. I am very proud."

Asa continued smiling, even though he didn't feel like it anymore. He pulled his hand away from Trunculin's as he walked off the balcony. His new guards were waiting for him. The fact that he was basically a prisoner had not changed. The guards were just nicer.

Trunculin stayed behind for a speech of his own about the details of the meeting with Extatumm. Asa could tell that he was annoyed. He had planned the speech to be at the same time Brenddel arrived, but so far, no Brenddel. It was supposed to be a brief speech, but Asa didn't want to hear it. He had said and heard enough lies for one day.

He was almost out of earshot when he sensed that the speech was going wrong somehow. Trunculin had stopped speaking and the sounds from the crowd were strange. Asa stopped and decided to go back and see what was going on. As he got closer to the balcony, he heard the crowds gasp.

When Asa was back on the balcony, he could see that everyone was looking in the same direction. There were two airships coming in, but something was clearly wrong. One airship was much larger than any he had ever seen. It was clearly not one of their airships. The shocking knowledge that someone else had airships, and that they were larger than their own, put the crowd in a strange mood.

The airships came in. The silver and black shape was enormous and covered the crowds in shadow. Brenddel's ship followed.

As they came and hovered near the balcony, Brenddel shouted down to the firstcouncilor. "Send every healer to the landing pads. We have many dead and wounded."

Before anyone could respond, the two airships were headed for the pads. Trunculin sent several guards to retrieve the healers. Asa looked at the firstcouncilor's face for any sign of what he was thinking. This time, Trunculin was not trying to hide his rage.

Chapter 18

Coated in Sweet Salt

The stolen airship hovered just outside the mountain range for some time. Mantuan wanted to make sure that they were not being followed. He was confident that Brenddel would fulfill his mission and deliver TrTorrin to the kingdom, but he could not afford to take any chances. Better to wait here and be attacked by a single damaged ship, than lead them back to the fortress. After enough time had passed, Mantuan was satisfied. They made their way to Aspora.

Mantuan attended the rest of the crew. There were only two men wounded. He assigned that to good planning and a great deal of luck. He wanted to imagine the expression on the firstcouncilor's face when the airships came home loaded with the dead and wounded. But there will be time for that later. Now, he needed to go check on Gordon.

Aline and Gordon spoke quietly as Mantuan walked up and sat with them. "Thank you Mantuan, all of you. I was sure I was going back to my death," Gordon said, "How did you know I'd be there?"

Aline smiled, "We have friends in surprising places."

Mantuan asked, "Thank the gods you're alive. How are you feeling? Did they hurt you?"

"I'm fine. I'm a little wobbly after all that's happened. They didn't hurt me. I was a prisoner, but they treated me well. It's strange that being taken prisoner was the first time I've had to actually rest since

I became king. I guess I didn't realize how tired I was. And no real sweetblood attacks, thankfully."

Aline added, "He was just telling me that his first airship ride didn't go too well."

Gordon laughed. "No, this airship ride is much better."

"I'm sorry that I let them take you. That will never happen again," Mantuan stated.

Aline chimed in. "And I won't leave your sight again, my king, no matter what Manny orders."

Mantuan almost said something to Aline, but decided to let the nickname go. "What did you do there?"

Gordon replied, "It was strange. The father came to my room a lot, even took me around the capital city. He was very proud of it. But I still don't understand why he was treating me so nicely or why they took me at all."

"I think it was to show how powerful they were, a negotiating point with Trunculin. And a way to say 'we easily captured one of your kings,'" offered Mantuan.

Gordon considered it. "Maybe. But I kept getting the feeling that he was trying to convince me of something."

"Like what?" asked Aline.

"Well, he talked about the fact that all of his people were equal and that because they all work for each other and share everything, that their system was fairer than ours."

"Equal? Everyone's the same there?" asked Aline with a bitter laugh.

"That's the way he made it sound. Everyone got the same kind of place to live and the same share of food ... kind of. But I saw a place where their workers went to one side of the building and the people that ran the kingdom went to another side of the building. I don't think they were eating the same thing," said Gordon.

"How did they explain that?" Mantuan asked.

Gordon answered, "His assistant tried. He said that the councilor's jobs were more important since they ran everything."

Aline said, "That doesn't sound equal."

"It kind of made sense when he was explaining it. Like, when I asked the father how they were all equal, but they still have a leader."

"I would wager that he said that he would relinquish his power *eventually*," Mantuan said.

Gordon was surprised. "He did. How did you know?"

Mantuan replied, "Men that overthrow other leaders have said this throughout history. 'This old leader was bad or corrupt, so I had to throw him out and take his place. But it's only for a little while.' Eventually, they will say, 'soon I can relinquish my power, just not yet.' Many men have said the same thing. And they always stay in power until they, themselves, are removed."

"But the father made it sound like it was a new idea, and that what they were doing had never been tried before."

Mantuan nodded. "And he probably truly believes that. We have heard rumors that they started destroying all of the old buildings, and all of the old statues. Is that true?"

"There were a few old buildings, but most of them looked pretty new. The statues were still there, but they all looked like TrTorrin, and then there was one big statue of their founder. They had one place where they kept a lot of old things."

Mantuan asked, "There's an answer. Why destroy the past? One answer is to make a point that the past is dead and they are in charge of 'the future.' Another reason is that the past can be dangerous. If you destroy the past, then you can claim that your idea is new, no matter how many times it has actually failed. One building with old things can do little harm, but they would have to destroy larger symbols of the past. Then they could say it never really happened."

Aline asked, "Did you meet anybody that disagreed with their ideas?"

"No," said Gordon. "But the tours I had were with the father or his assistant. I never really talked to other people."

Aline continued. "So no one that lives under their rules to tell you the truth? Makes sense. So you didn't go outside of the capital? You were only allowed to see what they wanted you to see. They didn't show you people living like animals? Worked to death? You saw no one beaten, no one going hungry?" Aline seemed to be getting angry.

"No. the father said that no one goes hungry. The reason they set their kingdom up the way they did was to make sure everyone was taken care of…"

Aline interrupted, growing angrier. "So he didn't tell you about the prisons, the ones far away from the capital? Where anyone that disagrees with him goes to die? He didn't show you how they work their prisoners like slaves at the gas fields?"

"Why are you getting so angry? What do you know about their land? How do you know their system doesn't work? The way the father … TrTorrin described it. Well, it sounded pretty good, in some ways. He said they just needed to fix a few problems."

Mantuan said, "Gordon, when you get rid of everyone that disagrees with you, and give the people just enough to live on, so that all they worry about is surviving, it makes it very easy to control the population. And when you totally control the people, you can make them believe anything you want. Listen to yourself, you seem to believe what TrTorrin was selling."

"I don't … I mean, it just sounded like a different way of doing things. I guess, some of his ideas did get in my head. But why so angry, Aline? You've never been there."

Aline didn't say anything. She just stared into Gordon's eyes.

Mantuan said softly, "She was born there, Gordon."

Gordon's mouth fell open. "But you said you were from Aspora."

"I would never claim that evil place as my home. I was taken out secretly when I was a baby. My mother and father weren't so lucky."

"I don't understand. You seem to hate your mother."

"Sandrell is one of the bravest women I've ever known," said Aline. "We have our differences, to be sure. But those people you speak so highly of took over the kingdom of Dard and killed the king and most of the royal family. The queen was able to escape. She found a new home with her granddaughter in Thure. But they killed everyone in the family, Gordon. Including the children."

Gordon sat there, not knowing what to say.

Aline continued. "My father and mother were warriors fighting his takeover. I learned to fight because of their example. TrTorrin killed my father. My mother survived and realized she needed to get me to safety. There was a small band of people that smuggled a few of us out. Because my mother was a leader, she couldn't just disappear. We got out and took refuge in Aspora. But my mother was caught and sent to prison after their 'glorious transformation' of Dard."

"I had no idea. How did she escape?" asked Gordon.

"They had her at the gas fields by then. She told me she'd been planning escape since she arrived. She had help. Terrible things happened there before she escaped. Maybe she will tell it to you about it someday, but I won't."

"The stories she tells of what happened in that place are awful." said Mantuan, "Her only crime was disagreeing with TrTorrin's new vision of the world."

Gordon was shocked. He was immediately ashamed that he had almost believed what the father had said, as a prisoner being told lies. *Why did I almost defend him?*

"They were not your friends, Gordon. They quietly fed you some bad ideas coated in sweet salt. They showed you a pretty picture of how things are there. But underneath it, it's all rotten."

They had reached the borders of Aspora and were headed towards the forest. Gordon saw the beginning of a large canopy of trees. He had heard so much about this place, and he was excited to finally see the place where Mantuan had fallen to his death and into a new life. The fortress was hundreds of feet high, living up in the air. Gordon couldn't wait to try and figure out how it was done.

Aline said, "But enough of the past. There is amazing news, Gordon. Your ... well. maybe you should just see for yourself."

"I know a lot has happened to you since you became king," said Mantuan. "But a lot more has happened since we last saw you. Everything has changed."

Aline interjected. "Wonderful things, Gordon. There are big surprises waiting for you."

Chapter 19

Brenddel Attacks

Trunculin was thankful that the landing pads were cut off from public access. He knew what the people would think of this nightmare if they saw it up close. The two ships had landed and all of the healers had begun taking the injured to the healing rooms.

There were not many alive to attend. Most of the work was removing the dead. There were over forty people on all of the air ships when they left Extatumm. Now, there were just nine left alive, besides Brenddel and TrTorrin. Five of them were wounded and two of them were not expected to survive the night.

Trunculin could only stare at the carnage and the blood on the decks. He knew it was bad timing, but he also marveled at the size and construction of the large Extatumm airship. The firstcouncilor turned his thoughts back to the moment. Trunculin did not like how far things had spiraled from his control lately. It was as though everything was turning against him.

Brenddel was busy barking orders and making sure everyone was taken care of. King Asa quietly stood by, watching. The young king felt numb as he watched the hurt and dead being moved. Trunculin felt just the opposite. He was enraged, but knew this was not the time to show it.

They were standing by a line of arched walkways, and Trunculin watched as the last of the victims was taken away. Besides Asa's guards, only TrTorrin, Brenddel, Trunculin, and the king remained. There was a fresh healer's cloth around the father's hand where Mantuan had cut him.

The father said, "King Asa, Firstcouncilor Trunculin, I had hoped to meet under better circumstances."

"Yes, we did too, TrTorrin. You had better go to the healing rooms to make sure that your hand is not worse than it looks," said Trunculin.

"Thank you, my hand is fine."

"I'm sorry, but I must insist," said Brenddel. "We cannot take any more chances. Small wounds can turn. My king, would you mind showing TrTorrin to the healing rooms? You can check on our men as well."

The father knew they wanted to talk alone. "Good King Asa. If you wouldn't mind leading the way?"

"Of course," said Asa as they walked away. "I suppose it would be a stupid question to ask how your trip was."

Now that they were alone, Trunculin's fury could not wait. He turned on Brenddel. "How could you let this ... " but before Trunculin could finish his question, Brenddel pulled Trunculin around a pillar and put his hand on Trunculin's throat. Trunculin's shocked eyes bulged out as he gasped for air.

Brenddel replied, "We were attacked by Mantuan and another airship. They took Gordon. They killed my men. How did they know we would be there?"

Brenddel released the firstcouncilor. He fell to the ground gasping. "How dare you. You ... "

But before Trunculin could object anymore, Brenddel yanked him back on his feet and this time had a shortknife to his throat.

Trunculin stopped talking and realized the danger of the situation. He composed himself and looked directly into Brenddel's eyes. With a voice as calm as he could, he said, "It wasn't me."

"Why should I believe that? There were only a handful of people that knew about this," said Brenddel.

"Put the knife away and think. I want this alliance. Why would I have the ships attacked? I wanted Gordon back. I have no control over what Mantuan does. Up until recently, I thought he was dead. You told me that you killed him, if you remember. Why were you attacked? I don't know. TrTorrin has nothing to gain. I have nothing to gain. This is a disaster, but not of my doing."

Brenddel reluctantly put his knife away and took a step back, staring deeply at the firstcouncilor. "All they wanted was Gordon. Why?"

"I have no idea, the boy has no value now. How did you even convince TrTorrin to bring Gordon back?"

"I didn't have to convince him. He was planning to bring him back as a present to you. It turned out to be a very expensive gift."

Trunculin pointed out. "You said one of the attacking ships was theirs. Why would they attack you? They already had Gordon. None of this makes sense."

"TrTorrin claimed that they had ships go missing," said Brenddel. "He says he assumed that they had gone down into the sea during test flights. It looks like someone has captured a few prizes from Extatumm."

"So Mantuan has been able to steal your airship and some of theirs as well? Quite the feat for a dead man."

"I saw him fall over the haunted forest. I can't imagine how he survived. It may not have been Mantuan that stole the Extatumm ships. The person on the stolen ship was Sandrell."

Trunculin froze. It took him a moment to speak, and Brenddel enjoyed watching the firstcouncilor's face change. He finally said, "Sandrell and Mantuan. I can't imagine a more dangerous partnership. And they have airships."

"They must have something bigger planned. They could have killed TrTorrin, but they didn't. They tried to kill me, maybe, but didn't. Why? Who else knew about our flight?"

"Only you, me, Asa, and TrTorrin. Why do they want Gordon so badly? He has been completely discredited and branded a coward. Even if he came back, people would call for his head. Why is Gordon important? Why make him king in the first place?" asked Trunculin, knowing that he would get no answers.

"I don't know, but now I go find Mantuan. I will take the fleet and kill him for good. I'll try to bring Gordon back alive, but no guarantees."

"Soon, I promise. We need to get through this treaty meeting, first."

"The more time that I waste, the further away they get, or the better they hide. Unless..." he wondered if he knew where Mantuan might be after all. He kept it to himself, "No delays. It must be now."

"Trunculin is right," said King Asa from behind them, having quietly returned from the healing room with his personal guards. They both turned around as Asa continued. "We must get this treaty done first. Then we will find them. Our men can't have died for nothing."

Since the king was agreeing with him, Trunculin didn't know what to say.

"As you wish, my king. I hope this alliance won't take too long," Brenddel said. "I would like to go check on my men in the healing rooms now, with your permission."

"Go ahead. Please keep me updated on their condition. Firstcouncilor, I think you and I should address the people. They will be anxious to know what just happened," said Asa.

Trunculin felt a confusing mix of emotions. He began to speak his mind and then looked at Brenddel's four best guards standing behind the king, and instead said, "I think that is wise, my king. Let me just write a speech ..."

"There's no time. Can't you hear the crowd from here? We'll go talk to them right now." Asa and the guards were walking back to the people before Trunculin had a chance to speak.

Trunculin walked quietly behind the guards, back to address the people. The entire way, he regretted not killing this particular king when he'd had the chance.

Chapter 20

Reunions

The airship was floating next to the edge of the vast forest. Straight down underneath the ship were steep, jagged cliffs. A few hundred feet down and away from their position was a small fleet of five airships. They looked much different than the airships Gordon was used to. They must be Extatumm ships, Gordon thought. *Why are Extatumm ships here?*

They were floating amid a haze of mist that clung to the cliff wall. Gordon could see the five ships were attached to ropes, but he could not figure out how the people got from those airships to the forest. *I have a lot to ask about.*

Gordon walked from the airship platform into the high village of the trees. Aline was ahead of Gordon and suddenly he was in a new world. Gordon's eyes didn't know where to look. There was so much to see. Small shafts of light from the canopy above showed platforms, stairs, and decks as far as he could see. There were hollowed out parts of trees and platforms around the trunks of others. A complex series of ropes and rope bridges hung among the trees almost like the web of a giant spider.

It was beautiful and strange and there were people everywhere. Gordon looked off one of the platforms and straight down. It really was hundreds of feet in the air, he told himself as he carefully walked back from the edge.

Mantuan was far ahead of them on another large platform, talking with a few of his people. Aline and Gordon came to Mantuan as he said, "Gordon, there is a lot to understand. So much has happened since you were taken. Just let the truth..."

Aline took Gordon by the hand. "He'll be all right, Manny. Gordon's strong," Aline led Gordon into a large room set in an enormous tree. Mantuan followed.

Gordon tried to concentrate on what was happening, but he also was distracted by the touch of Aline's hand. Strange feelings swirled in him. He was brought back to reality when he saw Denogg standing there. "Hello there, my boy."

"Denny?" Gordon's thoughts raced. If Denogg was here, did that mean...? And before he could finish his thought, he saw his Uncle Loren standing to one side. He rushed to Loren and hugged him tightly. Loren hugged him back. Gordon asked, "But how did you get out? I was worried you were already..."

"Dead? And I thought you were dead. I found out you were alive just as I found out you were also taken. But that doesn't matter now, we're both here." Loren looked seriously into Gordon's eyes and said, "This will be very strange, Gordon. But I need you to meet someone."

Gordon turned his attention towards a very pretty woman about Loren's age. She offered him a strange smile and he thought he could see a tear forming in her eye. Not wanting to be rude, he went over to her and offered his hand. "Hello. My name is Gordon."

She took his hand and put her other hand over her mouth. Gordon saw a tear drop.

"Uncle Loren, how did you meet someone while you were in prison?" asked Gordon innocently.

Everyone laughed.

Loren finally said, "It's nothing like that, I promise you. Gordon, this is Queen Ellice."

Gordon continued with his hand in hers, and suddenly there was a spark of recognition. "Oh... it's nice to meet you. Forgive me, my queen, but I had read that you were, well, dead."

Mantuan said, "There is a lot of that going around."

The room laughed again, but quieted down quickly.

Loren put his hands on Gordon's shoulders. "Yes, Gordon, we all thought she was dead until just recently. Gordon, Ellice is my sister. And she is your mother."

Gordon felt a tingle come over him, but then he pulled his hand away and said, "What? What do you mean? You ... you said my mother was dead."

Loren tried to comfort Gordon. "We all thought she was dead, son..."

"Son? I'm not your son. You... you lied to me. I'm... Wait. Does that mean my father was king Daymer? The slaver king?" said Gordon as he wheeled around the room. "I don't understand! You all lied to me!"

Aline stepped in and put her hands firmly on either side of Gordon face. "I know this is hard, Gordon, but we are not your enemy. We all just risked our lives to save you. We just found out that your mother was alive while you were gone. *But she is your mother.*"

Tears came down Gordon's eyes. He couldn't stop them. He wasn't sure from what emotion they flowed: love, anger, fear, or relief. Aline let go of Gordon and he looked at the woman again. He didn't know what to say to her.

Ellice stood there as well, not knowing what to do until somehow, finally they were in each other's arms. They both cried and somehow he knew that it was true. They stood there a long time. The rest of the room was quiet until the embrace naturally broke on its own. Questions flooded into Gordon's mind. "I don't understand. How... how could you be...? Loren said you ...? Did you just leave me?"

"Oh no, Gordon," said Ellice. "You have to understand that I thought you were dead. I thought you and Loren had both died in a terrible fire. I couldn't imagine how you survived. And Loren thought I had died. There's a lot to find about each other. Please, sit and we will talk about everything."

"Mind if I join you?" asked Aline's mother Sandrell, as she stood at the doorway. Aline rushed to her and jumped on Sandrell. The embrace lasted for a long time. Suddenly, the room was full of mothers and their children.

Mantuan and Aline described going to the mountains to find the lawkeeper and whom they found instead. Loren and Denogg told him how the queen of Thure released them, and Gordon relayed his experience in the lands of Extatumm. Sandrell explained that she had been capturing airships from Extatumm's fleet and had been coordinating with Mantuan.

"This is all so hard to believe," said Gordon.

Aline replied, "That's true. If we told our stories to anyone else, they probably wouldn't believe us."

The room was full of laughter. It was like all the dark clouds they'd all lived under were lifted.

"How long have you been planning this?" asked Gordon?

Mantuan replied, "I knew Trunculin had to be taken down the moment I flew off that airship. I've been finding allies and planning this since that day. Sandrell has been doing the same since she realized what Brenddel and Trunculin were doing in secret. The planning has been going on since you were born, Gordon."

Gordon's mother Ellice chimed in. "It seems we have all been planning things since our deaths. The world thinking I was dead did allow a new kind of freedom to find out what Trunculin was doing."

"I still don't exactly understand what he is planning. Why make an alliance with Extatumm? I thought Trunculin just wanted to control our kingdom," said Gordon.

Denogg replied, "At first, so did we. That was our goal, to get Trunculin out and restore the kingdom to the way it should have been all along. The queen of Thure gave us a very interesting letter about what she and her allies were planning. When she released us, we came straight here to make plans with Mantuan."

"She said she would furnish all the details later, and that she had to get us out of Thure," explained Loren. "We just narrowly escaped. I wish I'd seen Trunculin's face when those lights went out in the harbor."

Denogg confirmed. "I have a lot of friends at the docks of Thure and they were kind enough to allow us to escape by snuffing all the lights in the harbor at the same time."

"But the biggest thing I still don't understand," Gordon said, "is why make me the king?"

Mantuan sighed and replied, "That was my doing. And I hope you will forgive me for it. My plan was to put you on the throne, then reveal your true parents after we had publically exposed all of Trunculin's lies. I thought you were more protected than you were. I didn't think Trunculin would poison you. No one could predict you collapsing on stage. I had Aline in the palace and a few others, but I am so sorry that you were in such grave danger. It is the last time I make that mistake."

Gordon continued, "And how did Trunculin convince everyone that the king and queen were responsible for the slavery in the gas fields?"

The queen replied, "Trunculin is a powerful master of deceit. He knew that he might get caught, so he forged paperwork with the king's signature and used that as proof against us to the people of the kingdom. We could not dispute this, of course, because your father had already been killed and I had fled with Loren's help. Then Trunculin's men found us and thought they'd finished us off. As it turned out, all three of us actually survived. We just didn't know it until now."

"So what happens next?" asked Gordon.

They all looked at each other. Mantuan replied, "We have a plan. It is complex and dangerous for everyone. Some of us may not survive. But in the end, we will have taken down the ability of Extatumm and Trunculin to bring war on other kingdoms. We will permanently disable the airships of the father, and we will take down the firstcouncilor for all the people to see. We will return you to your kingship, the post that your father so proudly held before you, and restore your parents' reputation."

There was silence for a moment as it all sank in.

"Is that all?" asked Denogg, and everybody laughed again.

After the laughter died down, Mantuan said, "Ready to be assigned your roles in this war?"

Chapter 21

Brenddel's Story

"Can I steer?" asked King Asa.

"You can do anything you like, you are the king," said Brenddel as he handed the wheel to Asa. "Here. You need to be gentle with it, but firm at the same time. This ship has a lot of power, but it turns very easily. Do you see?"

Asa took the wheel of the airship. He turned to the right and the entire ship moved.

Asa said, "Whoa. Here, you... you take the wheel back."

But Brenddel just put his hands over Asa's to steady the ship. "Just like this, my king. That's better. Just keep it steady," said Brenddel as he removed his hands. The ship held steady with the young king in control.

"I can't believe I'm really doing this!" said Asa.

"I can't believe that you convinced Trunculin to allow you to go. I know you are the king, but we both know how things really are."

"True. Thanks, Brenddel. You are the only one that's honest with me," said Asa. "I didn't have to do much to talk him into it. I think Trunculin was glad to get rid of me once I signed the treaty. Maybe he hopes I die in battle. I think he only wanted me for the speech and that quick meeting in front of the crowds with TrTorrin."

"Which was very good. You're certainly growing into your kingship, even though your formal training has been interrupted."

"It seems like it's never going to get a proper start. Do all kings start this way? With crazy things happening all the time?" asked Asa.

Brenddel actually laughed. Asa had never heard this before. "Since you became king, things have been decidedly *not* normal."

"It's really true that Gordon's alive? And he was taken by this Mantuan guy?"

"Yes, my king," Brenddel said rushing forward again. "But you have to keep it steady. Like this. Yes, Gordon and Mantuan are alive."

Asa steered for another moment. Brenddel could sense that he wanted to ask a question, but hesitated. Finally he said, "Are we going to kill them?"

"Mantuan, yes. Others, only if we have to. We will take as many prisoners as we can, including Gordon. But Mantuan will not come back alive, my king. That is certain," replied Brenddel, losing his smile.

Asa asked, "So, it's true that Mantuan killed the king? The one that made the slaves work at the gas fields? I heard about it from one of my teachers. He didn't seem to want to talk about it."

"No," Brenddel replied, "I killed the king."

Asa jerked the ship again and he stabilized it quickly, but Brenddel called the pilot back over so they could talk somewhere more private.

"You killed the king? But you're a good man. Why would you do that?"

"Thank you for saying that, my king. That means, in your service so far, I have conducted myself honorably. But I am not a good man. I'm a man who gets things done. The king had to die."

"I don't understand. Why?"

"Mantuan was the firstman of the kingdom and King Daymer was loved by all the people. Even the two councils liked him. He was fair, just, and kind to all the soldiers and all of his people. He was almost too good to be true."

"What do you mean?"

"I was born in Artoth," Brenddel explained. "I lived there with my parents when I was a small boy. My parents left me during the war of Asgonan, the large island between Extatumm and Artoth. When my parents abandoned me, Mantuan found me and became my new father. He trained me as a warrior. In time, I become his secondman. It was the best time to serve the kingdom, since Daymer was the best king. We had just began building our fleet of airships. We connected the entire world with trade and goods. It was a bright world that the king promised." Brenddel paused.

"I'm sorry, Brenddel. You don't have to talk about if you don't want to."

"No, my king, you asked an honest question, and I want to give you an honest answer. It is not a good thing to kill a king. But I would do it again after what I found out."

"You mean the slaves at the gas fields?" asked Asa, trying to remember the details of the stories he had heard.

Brenddel nodded. "It was I who first suspected something was wrong. That's the strangest thing. I think, in a way, that Mantuan and the king almost wanted to get caught, because Mantuan sent me on missions to the fields. I was sent to make sure that the ships were being built on time and the gas fields were running like they should."

"Mantuan *sent* you there, even though he knew you might find something?"

"Yes. The king wanted a fleet built as quickly as possible. But every time I went to the fields, there were more and more workers. Then I started to talk to people that actually worked at the gas fields. When I asked where all of the workers came from, they seemed panicked."

King Asa waited patiently. Brenddel had never talked about himself. Asa was just glad to spend time with Brenddel, but he could tell this was painful for him.

"I confided my fears to Mantuan and he became very disturbed. He said he would talk to the king. Trunculin came to me and told me that the king and Mantuan have been plotting something for a long time, but he didn't know what. He suggested that I quietly go back and do another inspection of the gas fields myself, but without them knowing. So I went back for a surprise inspection. This time, I saw horrible things. The people in charge were all corrupt. I saw how the workers were being treated. The people that were from our kingdom were being paid for their work. But there was another kind of worker, people that came from other kingdoms. They were being used as slaves."

King Asa did not know what to say. He was surprised at how emotional Brenddel was getting as he continued.

"One woman kept looking at me. She was constantly coughing, obviously very sick. But she kept looking. She asked me where I was from and I told her. She burst into tears and asked more questions. I was a small boy when my parents disappeared. The moment she touched my face, and I looked into her eyes, I knew she was my mother."

"Your mother? Your mother was working as a slave? You mean … you mean she hadn't abandoned you? She'd been taken as a slave to the gas fields?"

"Very good, my king. You understood that quickly. I did not. I brought her back secretly, but the healers could not do much to help her. She was very sick and she died only two days later. Only after she died, did all of the pieces start fitting together in my mind. There were waves of understanding that came over me in the following days. I realized it was no coincidence that Mantuan was in Artoth at the same time my parents suddenly disappeared. Trunculin and I became convinced that they'd been using the airships to find slaves for the king."

"That's awful. What did you do? How did you confront Mantuan?"

"After realizing that my adoptive father betrayed me, I knew I could trust no one. I turned to the firstcouncilor who had insisted I inspect those fields. If I hadn't, I never would've known. But while I was at the fields, Trunculin discovered the larger plot. He was the one that showed me documents signed by Mantuan and the king, with my parents' names as slaves."

"What happened to your father?"

"He died a few years before I found my mother. Trunculin told me that the king and Mantuan suspected that their plans had been discovered. Trunculin was afraid of them. He thought we needed to help fate and kill them for the crimes they committed. At first I wanted them to stand trial in front of everyone, but Trunculin was sure they would find a way to convince everyone that we were the guilty ones. Trunculin feared Mantuan might kill him under the king's order. I was convinced we had to act first."

The pilot informed them that they were close to the gas fields. Brenddel nodded to him and continued. "Trunculin convinced the king that there was a new alliance to be made. We arranged to go to Aspora. It was a quiet, secluded place to take care of the problem. We were over a forest of giant trees that only grow in that land. Just before we got to the forest, I took care of the slaver king. He was looking over the land, and I came up behind him. I whispered to him that he was dying as punishment for my parents. I stabbed him and he fell over the side. I had made sure all the men on board were loyal to me that day, even the healer that had tried to save my mother. No one interfered, except Mantuan. We fought. Me with my longknife and Mantuan with his battle-axe. A few times I thought he was going to beat me, but my rage fueled me. I finally bested him and he fell off the airship into the trees," said Brenddel. "I kept his axe."

"How did Mantuan survive that? How high up were you?"

"I don't know how he lived. The trees are hundreds of feet high. He should have died, but obviously he survived. He won't survive again."

"Is that where we're going? To look for him in Aspora, in that forest?"

They were just beginning to land. There was a crew on the ground as the men dropped the ropes to secure the ship.

Brenddel replied, "Yes. I have a strong feeling he's there. Where else would a dead man go but the haunted forest? He will die there and be a true ghost."

"Yes. He will," the king said firmly.

"Welcome to your gas fields, my king. Let me show you to your fleet. There is a special ship I think you will like."

Asa was shown around. It was a vast network of buildings, machines and pipes. Brenddel explained how they separated the gas, but Asa didn't really understand it all. He was too busy looking as the large machinery. Brenddel showed Asa to the new airship that had just been finished.

Asa stared at the giant ship. Brenddel smiled as the king stared. "It's huge!" Asa surprised Brenddel by asking, "Can we name it?"

"Name the ship? I suppose. We usually only give them numbers, but you are the king."

"We will call it," Asa looked at Brenddel seriously, "the Justice."

Brenddel thought of his parents and nodded his approval. They walked onto the deck of the new airship.

Chapter 22

Win or Lose

"All quiet. The Firstcouncilor Trunculin has called together the meeting of these two great councils for introduction of treaty between our great kingdom and the people of Extatumm. All rise."

Both councils were assembled before them. Trunculin walked out to speak, and TrTorrin came out next to him. Trunculin knew this had to go well for the councils to approve the treaty. Back room chatter often got in the way. If it was not decided here and now, the firstcouncilor knew that the idea was dead.

Trunculin began. "Members of both councils, we come before you with the treaty between our two great peoples, signed by King Asa, for you to consider. Before I go on, I would just like to take a moment to welcome our most honored guest, Alonnia, grandmother to the queen of Thure."

The grandmother had arrived earlier in the day. She rose to thunderous applause from all the council members.

Trunculin continued. "It is our hope that this treaty signed in good faith by the Father of Extatumm, and by good King Asa, will bring a new understanding between us. Long have we railed against their new ideas. Ways that many thought were a challenge to our system of kingdom. But now that there's been a long stable period of time, and the dust of history has finally settled in the distant lands, it is clear that we must deal with reality as it is. I know I speak for the king when I say that there are great things we can learn from each other."

Much of the chamber erupted in applause. It was the vast majority of councilors, and many stood, but Trunculin made a mental list of those that did not. When the applause died down, Trunculin motioned for the father to speak.

TrTorrin began. "Thank you. You don't know what that applause means to a humble man who was born the son of a farmer, far from the capital where I now live. And after thousands of years of men living the same way, we have found a different path. Until now, our new ideas have been shunned and mocked by many kingdoms. But with this alliance today, and your full support, my people can finally rejoin the world. This treaty will shine a light on our new system of doing things. And in return, perhaps the light of our new ways will shine on the rest of the world."

More applause rose, and many councilors stood. But a great number did not stand or even applaud. The grandmother sat there, silently, with her hands in her lap. She did not scowl at the father. She simply did not look at him at all.

The secondcouncilor approached the speaking platform. "The two sides have made their statements and the treaty has been posted for all to see. There will be a short period for questions. Then there will be a vote by both chambers, barring a motion to postpone this decision."

Trunculin knew that both councils voting now was the only way. There was a short question and answer period. He would have to endure it. Trunculin was just glad the questions were limited to a set amount of time.

Many councilors stood to ask questions. *More than I expected,* thought Trunculin. He knew they would never get through the forty or so questions in time. He chose the closest councilor to him. "Yes, you there. Your question?"

"The most obvious one. How can we trust them?" asked the councilor.

Trunculin replied, "There are no grounds for your question. For all the hatred that they have endured, by our kingdom and others, the people of Extatumm have never attacked another kingdom or forced their way of life on anyone else." the councilor sat and Trunculin chose another in the crowd. "You, there."

Without standing, a councilor asked, "What about the war of Asgonan?"

Trunculin said, "That was a few battles over an island that was in dispute, not a proper war. It is settled history between Extatumm and Artoth. You, there."

"This question is for the father. The firstcouncilor claims you never forced your new way of life on anyone. Didn't you force this new system on all the people of Dard when you killed those that would not convert?"

There was great applause, and several members of the chamber roared their approval.

"There are many stories that have come out of our land," the father said, smiling broadly. "But many of them are just legends. We tried to start peacefully with our new ideas. Since these ideas did not include our ruling family, it was they that made war on us. We simply defended ourselves. Since we had the people and the workers on our side, we defeated them. We didn't want this war, but after winning it, there was no turning back."

Trunculin did not like the way this was going, but he had no choice but to continue. He just hoped that his secret campaign of bribes and intimidation behind the scenes ultimately worked. *This will be over soon*, he hoped. "Yes, councilor."

"Also for the father. Is it true that your land has abolished hunger, and there are no poor in your lands?" Trunculin was relieved for a friendly question.

"Yes, councilor, it is true. Because we have brought equality to all of our people, everyone has enough to eat. No one starves. We have also done away with most sicknesses that afflict other kingdoms. Everyone has what they need."

"You, councilor," said Trunculin.

"So you deny that there are thousands, even millions of people that have died since you took over because of your new, 'glorious' system?"

The father did not smile, but wore a mask of sadness instead. "Unfortunately, people have died, but no more than would have died otherwise. Since we transformed into Extatumm, we had the worst drought and the worst winter in our history."

"Don't you see that the gods are punishing you?" asked someone else without standing.

The father smiled. "No. No offense to other kingdoms, but we have done away with the superstitions of the past. We look only to ourselves for the answers."

Another asked, "And how full are your prisons? Is it not true that you lock away anyone who disagrees with you?"

Trunculin was about to stop the question, but the father answered. "No. That is not true. There are many that want to live in the past, and refuse to acknowledge the future as it unfolds. We have simply found the answers a little faster than other kingdoms. Our system is the natural conclusion of history. That's why I hope to make alliances. To dispel the lies and show other kingdoms what we have learned, and how we have found a new way to live that makes everybody truly equal," explained TrTorrin. "I think you are referring to our enlightenment camps. They are not prisons. They are places where the people who refuse to see are taught how to open their eyes. Once we believe that they fully understand and accept our new way of life, they are reintroduced into our people."

There were grumbles amongst the entire chamber, and Trunculin did not like it. He decided to do some damage control and call the councilor he knew was on his side. "Yes, councilor, what is your question?"

The councilor smiled and gave a little nod to Trunculin. He asked, "Isn't it true that you have built a vast army of airships based upon plans you received from us? Were the plans stolen from us or were they sold to you? And who will you attack first with them?" the councilor finished and looked at Trunculin, still smiling, giving a second nod to underscore the point that he no longer belonged to Trunculin.

The firstcouncilor's eyes shot fire as he stared at the councilor whom he had bribed earlier that day, "How dare you accuse our guest…"

The father waved off Trunculin and said, "No. I will answer. We have neither stolen nor been sold any plans to airships. But I cannot lie. Seeing your great airships for so many years inspired our thinkers to try and copy your great airships designs. Unfortunately, the airship I brought with me is our only success. Since we don't have the same way to get the lifting gas that your kingdom has, our ability to emulate your greatness has been a failure for the most part … but I will admit that I brought our only airship to show off a little."

A few people in the chamber laughed.

Another councilor stood and began to speak without Trunculin calling on him. "Is it true that you took our ex-King Gordon, captured and interrogated him? Isn't it true that you were attacked and Gordon was taken from you? Isn't that how our guards died?"

The chamber erupted with shouts, just as the secondcouncilor called, "Time!"

"The time for debate is over," said Trunculin, relieved. "But I am appalled and embarrassed for any councilor who would stand and accuse our guest of such ridiculous things. I only wish we had more time to prove that those questions were infested with lies. As it stands, we must ignore that poisonous last question."

The secondcouncilor said, "Members of both councils, do you agree to accept this treaty in good faith. If so, please stand."

Trunculin saw with horror only a handful of councilors stood. He noted that he was bribing them all. Many others that he thought he owned only sat and stared at him.

The secondcouncilor swallowed hard, afraid to ask, "All those opposed, please stand." A large wave of councilors rose from their chairs, saying nothing.

The secondcouncilor slowly stated, "The measure whether to adopt this treaty as written and signed by the king..." he cleared his throat, "...fails."

There was much applause as nearly every councilor stood, all staring at Trunculin. Only a few very loyal to Trunculin stayed seated and silent, looking around and trying to hide their fear.

The grandmother sat in her seat, smiling.

The father nodded courteously and walked out. Trunculin surveyed the councilors and imagined the room filling up with fire as he left the chamber.

Trunculin and the father went back to the firstcouncilor's chamber. Drinks in hand, the father said, "Not what I'd hoped for. Not what you promised. Those were very informed questions."

Trunculin agreed. "Yes. They seem to have surprisingly reliable information. They will soon find their families in very dangerous situations. I can't imagine who they have been talking to."

"True versions of reality have no place in the public's mind, especially not in the heads of those that would lead them. They need to be told what they think. I thought you knew that."

"I do. Believe me when I say I am much older and wiser than you. With my absence in Thure, the whispers have grown louder. Now that I'm back, the whispers will stop, or be put to the knife."

"The knife is an excellent cure for whispers," said the father. "Speaking of knives, I am sorry we couldn't kill Gordon for you."

"Pardon? I don't understand."

"In Thure, I have agents there in some of the important social houses," explained TrTorrin. "They were instructed to kill important figures visiting Thure. It was only by mistake that the King of Thure drank from Gordon's cup."

"It was you!" said Trunculin. "But why kill visiting dignitaries, and not the king?"

"Hard to purposely poison a king or queen in their own lands. Most kings have people to taste their food. I was just lucky. My plan was to make Thure unworthy of trust. If important visitors started dying in Thure, people would stop visiting and Thure would become more isolated. It was only by chance that he picked up Gordon's cup. Sorry I didn't fix that problem for you."

"Why didn't you kill him when you had him in Extatumm?"

TrTorrin didn't answer, but smiled and raised his glass.

Trunculin smirked. "Ah, he was more valuable as a bargaining chip with me."

A guard came into the chamber and whispered to Trunculin. "That is fine," Trunculin said to the guard, and the guard left.

"It seems that the old Queen of Dard wishes an audience," said Trunculin.

The father put his cup down and got ready to leave when the first-councilor said, "An audience with both you and myself."

The father looked vaguely surprised by this, but nodded his acceptance. The Grandmother entered as though she was still the Queen of Dard, using her cane, but still very regal.

"Efeta ladd entedium," said the father smoothly.

"Andelott ent Yulios," replied the Grandmother. "I see you still remember how to address a queen of Dard properly."

The father replied, "I remember all of the old ways. Even my years in prison at your orders, my former queen."

She sat down in a chair, in front of them both, wasting no time. "Now that the vote is done, and you have lost, what are your plans, monster?"

The father replied, "Why, merely to return to my lands and find the next place I can make a treaty. Perhaps I will start closest to us at the kingdom of the gods. I wonder if the two kings would accept."

"Do you remember the last time we met?" asked the grandmother.

The father smiled nostalgically and simply nodded.

The Grandmother turned to Trunculin. "The last time we met was just after the final battle. It was clear that we would have to go into exile. My husband and I had many relatives fighting these ... people. Many had died. Some family lived in other kingdoms. The king and I were caught and brought before the two fathers at the time. The other father made a most unfortunate end. I wonder what Ollander said to make you kill him?"

She looked at TrTorrin again who said nothing, simply listening. She continued. "TrTorrin slit my husband's throat in front of me, but said he would let me live … that he wanted me to be in exile and to get old so that every other kingdom could see how the idea of kings and queens is old, and how it should die in disgrace."

The father sat still, looking at the queen. Trunculin did not know what to say or what to make of this visit, but the Grandmother continued. "But that is the past. I'm concerned now about my granddaughter. She believes that you, monster, plan to install Darion as king, by force if necessary."

The father smiled. "We have no current issue with your kingdom. My next concern is the kingdom of the gods. Your kingdom has no wealth or resources that we care about. We're not interested in old statues and old records of days gone by. And we are not in the business of installing new kings. We are the ones that throw kings and queens out of the lands they *think* they own. Does that satisfy you?"

"The only thing that would satisfy me would be to see you hanging upside down from the Gates of Dard. Of course, they're not the gates that I remember. I have heard of what you've done to them, which was the same thing you did to everything in my land. You destroyed anything that did not fit with your view of the world. All you can do is destroy, monster. I believe you worship destruction. But I'm just an old woman with no power. I will relay the message to my granddaughter. Goodbye, firstcouncilor. Goodbye, monster."

She stood and breezed out of the room.

The father smiled. "What a woman. The real reason I didn't kill her that day was because I admire her strength. She's still a great lady. Now, if you'll excuse me, Trunculin, the treaty has failed and I must leave."

"Yes. I understand."

The father walked out and was gone. Trunculin finished his drink and started to ponder what was happening. He suddenly felt very old. Was it really possible to fail after all of the time and planning? No, he told himself. Trunculin decided that he would start on his list right away. There were many councilors to be quietly killed and replaced. It would be a long list for Brenddel's men when he got back from killing Mantuan. The thought cheered him up, but first he would have to see the mystics for a while.

* * *

Just outside the kingdom of the thirteen, the father's airship came in low and hovered over the water. On board his watership, Darion was absentmindedly flipping a king's coin. On one side was his brother's face. The other side showed the great port of Thure. Darion boarded the airship and asked, "Did it go well?"

The father replied, "It went as expected. Time for the next step."

Darion smiled. They flew off, and headed back to Extatumm.

The war had begun.

Chapter 23

Secret Meeting

The firsthealer Corinn, had better things to do. Trunculin had given her strict instructions to make the wounded soldiers from the airship her first priority. Of course, she had done her duty, but not for Trunculin. She took her job very seriously and that's why she was so annoyed when she got the note. She didn't have time for nonsense, but the note had intrigued her. First, it was left in her chambers, which were always locked when she wasn't there. No one else had a key. What the dangerous note said really caught her attention.

> *I believe you can help me.*
> *I know I can help you.*
> *It concerns a very* old *mutual friend of ours.*
> *He may take a fall. The wheels are already turning.*

The fact that one word was stressed made Corinn curious. If someone else knew what she only suspected, it wouldn't hurt for her to find out who it was, however hopeless. That Trunculin had such bold enemies, actually made Corinn smile. She followed the instructions on the bottom of the note about where to meet, and took her healing bag along in case she was noticed by any of Trunculin's agents. She quietly went to the king's dock and looked for the banner.

She spotted the two small triangle banners attached to a small, plain ship. They were subtle, but she took note that one was hanging right side up, while another was upside-down. A man met her as she came over the ramp and onto the ship. The man took the note from Corinn without a word, pointing to the stairs down into the ship. She saw the man tear up the note and fling it into the water as she descended into the dark ship.

Her breath caught in her throat as she met the eyes of the mystic. His eyes did not blink. But Corinn was more surprised when she saw the man who had sent her the note.

The man rose and bowed slightly. "Thank you for coming, firsthealer. I'm sorry to be so mysterious, but these are dangerous times, filled with dangerous people."

"True, I just didn't think you were one of them. Should I call you by a name or a title?"

"Just use the title 'friend.' And I'm only dangerous to one man."

"If he can be called that," offered the mystic, still staring at Corinn.

"I hope you are not trying to poke around in my mind," Corinn said. "Was it you that caused Gordon to collapse?"

The mystic showed no sign of emotion. "I was in his mind only briefly. I did not harm the boy. We believe he had something like a vision dream."

"What it might mean, is why you are here," the man said. "We have discovered many things about our mutual friend, including that he's been close to only one person in recent memory."

"Let's be clear. We are talking about Trunculin, and yes, we were close once. That is no one's business but mine and the firstcouncilor's."

"That is true, I'm not trying to pry into your private life. I am missing a piece of the picture. I can share certain information with you if you could fill in the gap. Trunculin is a very bad man."

"We all know that. You must have seen things yourself over the years, I certainly have. That's why Trunculin and I are no longer close. What is this really about?"

"Wars between all of the kingdoms at once, a world on fire. We believe that is Trunculin's goal. Or at least the next step in achieving his goal of total control," offered the mystic.

Corinn looked from the mystic to the man who had summoned her, and began to laugh.

The man said, "This is not a jest. Trunculin."

"No, it's not a jest," Corinn stopped laughing and became angry, "But who are you two? One of you has been helping him for years. Yes, mystic I know of the help you have given to Trunculin in your 'meetings.' You dare to say you want to bring him down now? And you, friend, whatever you call yourself now, you stood by him for years, doing nothing. Just playing your part, I suppose. How dare both of you!"

"Don't play the innocent. We all stood by while he concentrated his power, you helping control the kings. Yes, I know about that. I have been secretly collecting evidence for years against Trunculin. The mystics have stopped helping him, and you helped him only recently by poisoning Gordon so Trunculin could control him."

"I've heard enough," said Corinn, getting up to leave.

"Stay," the mystic said, standing. He gave a slight nod, still not blinking. "Please."

The man rose as well. "I'm sorry, Corinn. Trunculin's power grows when we are fighting. There are many of us working hard to bring him down. The plans have already begun. Those of us who know what he is need to work together. The wheels are in motion. We just need to know one thing."

Corinn slowly sat back down. "I know how powerful he is. So this is probably hopeless. But if there's a chance to stop him ... what do you want to know?"

The man asked the questions and shared his information. When it was all laid out, they agreed that they had enough proof to destroy Trunculin forever. They just needed the help of one more person to be sure.

Chapter 24

Battle of the Fortress

"Are you sure you're ready for this?" asked Mantuan.

"We're ready, just make sure you are. You know Brenddel's going to want blood," said Sandrell.

Mantuan replied, "I know. Remember, our friends in the kingdom say that at least half of the fleet will move out. Don't even try to land on the beach until then."

Sandrell nodded. "I just hope our secret weapons do what they claim they will do. If those men aren't there, this won't work."

"They'll be there," Mantuan said, but was interrupted by Aline jumping on him and hugging him. Mantuan hugged back and finally Aline let go.

"Take care, Manny. If you die ... well, I will be very mad at you."

Mantuan smiled. "We will see each other again. You take care of your mother."

Loren came up to Mantuan and said, "We just spotted a fleet coming our way. I don't think Brenddel is very happy with you. He brought a lot of airships."

"I just hope he brought my axe."

"Time to go," said Sandrell. They left the fortress and boarded their Extatumm airships through the well-hidden exit. They were gone long before Brenddel arrived.

Mantuan turned his attention towards the fleet. He climbed up the branch to a small hole in the canopy made just for lookouts. Mantuan spotted at least fifteen individual ships in the distance.

There was one ship larger than he had ever seen. Gordon popped his head up from the branch next to him, and Mantuan handed Gordon the spyglass.

"It looks like Brenddel is going to use his new toy," said Mantuan.

"Did you know that they had built something like that?" said Gordon, sounding alarmed.

"They've been talking about it for years, a great airship to hold more weapons and men. They are going to have a lot of arrows and lots of fire."

"Will the plan still work?" asked Gordon.

"Hmmm. I think so?" said Mantuan as he vanished back down under the canopy of trees.

"You think so?" said Gordon as he followed Mantuan down.

* * *

Brenddel and his fleet arrived near the forest.

"Are you sure they're here?" asked King Asa.

"No. But this is where Mantuan fell. How could a man fall three hundred feet through a forest and not die? Hopefully he will surrender and answer that question. This forest is said to be haunted. No one goes in and comes out again."

"You think Mantuan is a ghost?" asked Asa, excited at the idea.

"I think what haunts this forest is Mantuan's army. But we will make sure."

Let him use his one airship, Brenddel thought. Even Mantuan couldn't beat his numbers. He had brought many ships and an army of men.

Brenddel ordered the first wave of ground soldiers.

They descended from the ropes and made their way to the forest entrance with shield, small arrows and longknives.

Brenddel explained, "This is to confirm that they are in there and guess at their numbers, if possible. It's too dangerous to send an army into a forest that they know, and we don't."

King Asa replied, "Then our numbers wouldn't count for much, right?"

Brenddel looked at Asa. "Very good, my king. Exactly right."

Asa smiled shyly. "My studies are going a little better."

On the ground, the soldiers entered the forest cautiously. There were only a few clear paths in, and they knew it could be a trap. They entered looking in all directions. There were small trees and plants of all sizes, but rising above it all were the giant trees.

The soldiers had heard that they were hundreds of years old. They stretched up so high, that the soldiers could not see the tops. As the men looked up, there came a furious volley of arrows. None of the soldiers saw where they came from; most had no time to even put up their shields. When the volley was over, every man looked around for the source of the attack. Several men picked up arrows that had been shot at them. All of them had blunt heads, with no tips.

Suddenly, there came a booming voice that seem to come from everywhere and echoed throughout the forest. "Why send in scouts, Brenddel? You know I'm here."

Brenddel heard Mantuan's voice even high in his airship. He had no idea how Mantuan was doing it, but it was clearly his voice and it seemed to boom from all around.

Mantuan asked, "No answer? We don't want to hurt soldiers of the kingdom. Call them back now, and they will not be harmed. If you go forward with your attack, we will defend ourselves."

"Where's his voice coming from?" asked the king.

"I don't know," Brenddel said as he walked to the edge of the deck and shouted as loud as he could. "I will have all your men surrender. Give yourselves up and we will not attack." Brenddel had no way to know if Mantuan could hear him from this high up.

Mantuan's laughter boomed through the forest. Several flocks of birds lifted from the canopy trees. "Oh, is that all? I must decline. You are wrong about so many things, Brenddel. You will end up regretting this. Let no man die today."

Brenddel shouted again. "You earned this day. You should have stayed dead, Mantuan."

"Well, I'm back now," said Mantuan, "and I want my axe."

"It's right here. Come get it, old man. You'll have no use for it after I kill you again."

Brenddel ordered the first wave of five ships to slowly hover over the canopy of trees. All of their weapons were pointed at the canopy. The orders were to shoot at anything that moved.

The ships were in formation so that some were close to the canopy and others were far above it. Another small flock of birds exploded out of the canopy and one of the soldiers fired a small arrow. Several others on the ship instinctively fired along with the man before they realized it was just birds.

Before they had a chance to laugh about it, a small barrage of arrows erupted from the trees, directly at them. Most of the men near the railings were hit. Some fell overboard into the canopy of trees. A ship nearby saw this and fired several large arrows where they thought the attack had come from. It was almost as though the canopy of trees was like deep green waters.

Anything could be beneath them.

The ship that was firing large arrows was met with a barrage of small arrows as well, but this time some of the tips were on fire and some hit the men on the deck. The men lifted their arrow plates from the deck of the ship. This allowed them to fire directly down beneath them through the grate-like openings that made up the under-deck.

The ship's volley of arrows flew, but the problem was that they could not tell if they were hitting anything. Before they knew it, every ship was being attacked at the same time. The men on deck furiously tried to put out small fires erupting on deck from fire arrows. Brenddel was surprised they were using fire arrows; a very dangerous gamble in a flammable forest.

Brenddel watched as a large arrow came straight up out of the forest and punctured the deck of an airship. He could see that a large rope was attached to it. As soon as the arrow punctured the deck, the airship was pulled towards the canopy.

Have they built war machines? Thought Brenddel.

When it was about ten feet from the canopy, more large arrows flew and punctured the floating section of the airship until it simply fell, to rest on top of the canopy, all the floating gas gone from the ship.

It almost looked like a watership had landed on a green ocean of leaves. The trees were so thick that the airship remained laying on top of the leaves. But the unlucky men climbing out from under the ruined ship fell straight through to the forest below.

Brenddel did not know if they fell to their deaths or not. They may have survived like Mantuan had, or they may have been taken prisoner by the ghosts of the forest.

* * *

On the ground level of the forest, the foot soldiers were still making their way. The floor was covered with leaves, debris, and thick foliage they could barely see through. They heard birds calling and the sounds of other animals rustling.

They kept looking upward, expecting another attack of small arrows, but none came as they went forward. Then, a dozen men simply fell into the ground. The men still standing saw them drop out of existence.

The men cautiously got closer to where their fellow soldiers disappeared. At each spot, they saw what looked like a round tunnel going straight down. It was definitely made by men. It looked like smooth rock formed the opening. They had no way to know that on the far side of the forest, the men suddenly slid out of small, round tunnels. They flew out of the cliff's steep face to the valley below.

The soldiers in the forest were told not to retreat until they saw the first signs of fire, which meant that the last option had been taken. Looking everywhere for signs of fire, the leading soldiers thought they saw some sort of man-made addition to the trees, like bridges or walk-ways. It was so far up that it was hard to see. The men didn't have a chance to investigate. The leaves around them seemed to come to life, as men camouflaged in the forest took every last soldier down.

* * *

Outside the forest, from the large ship, Brenddel and King Asa could see the airships were being taken down one by one. The airships were covering such a large area of the forest that Brenddel could not even guess how many men Mantuan had. He realized it was a much larger number than he had expected.

The wind was blowing harder now, rustling the forest loudly. Brenddel saw the heavy gray clouds rolling towards them. He hoped the weather would hold long enough. He would finish this today, no matter what happened.

Mantuan's voice came from everywhere at once. "Sorry, Brenddel, it looks like your men inside my forest will not be joining you."

Brenddel shouted, "Coward! Stop hiding and face me. Don't make me burn you out!"

Mantuan's voice boomed from nowhere and everywhere. "I am sorry it came to this Brenddel. I hope you see the truth one day. Do what you think you have to, but when this is over you must follow the trail. Smoke leads to truth."

Brenddel shouted back, "Your trail leads to death, and your patch on my wall next to the axe."

But Mantuan did not answer again.

Brenddel could see that he had no choice but to send in the fire ships. He signaled, and the airships moved into position at a high distance. They knew that a forest fire was unpredictable and that the flames could easily shoot up to them.

As they were preparing to drop fire, large arrows came from every-where and attached themselves to the deck of all the ships hovering over the forest. Brenddel signaled for them to continue. He reasoned that the ropes would simply burn away when the fires began. There would be no time for them to drag all of the ships down before everyone in the forest burned.

The wind was definitely getting stronger, thought Brenddel. The clouds were rolling in faster, promising rain, but not before they drove Mantuan out. He watched as each ship released a column of fire down on the forest, which was instantly on fire in many areas at the same time, promising to spread.

Anyone in the forest would have nowhere to run. Mantuan would *have* to come out of the forest. Brenddel would easily capture all of his "ghost army." Either that, or they could jump from the steep cliffs on the other side of the forest.

The ropes were still attached to the airships, but there had been no attempt to pull any airships down. Something occurred to Brenddel about the ropes. He looked closer through his spyglass.

The ropes all appeared to be wet. *No*, he thought. He realized his mistake in ordering the fire so quickly and signaled for the men to cut the ropes. Most of them got the signal and tried to detach the ropes. Since Brenddel was so far away, many did not get the signal at all and kept pouring fire onto the forest. Brenddel saw many game animals fleeing the forest, but no men.

Brenddel watched, powerless, as he saw fire shoot up several of the ropes. The wooden decks immediately caught fire. He realized, too late, that the ropes were coated in oil. The forest might go up in flames, but so would most of his airships.

Chapter 25

The Extatumm Fields

Aline and Sandrell waited with their ragged fleet. There were seven waterships of all different types. They had put together their small fleet with anything their allies could scrounge: merchant vessels and fishing boats from anywhere and everywhere. Sandrell hoped it would be enough. They couldn't draw too much attention. They waited on the outer border of the Extatumm waters. The plan would work, thought Sandrell, unless there were extra patrol ships working in the outer waters. Sandrell's mind was focused on the mission. She went over it again and again. She only had one doubt.

Fortistaf.

No. I will not think of him. Surely someone's killed him by now. She shook off the thought and looked in the distance. Since they were far from the capital, they hoped to be well hidden. Even though they were miles away, they could see the airships assembled over the capital. Apparently, their informant had been correct. "No reason to assemble that many ships in one place unless you mean to go to war," Sandrell told Aline.

"Has anyone heard from the man we sent to Artoth?" asked Aline.

"No," Sandrell said grimly. "I fear that the kingdom of the gods didn't heed our warning."

"What is that?" asked Aline, "Is it…?"

"By the gods, I think it is. We should pray for Artoth, for all of us," said Sandrell as they saw a shape rising outside the capital. It rose like a deformed sun. It kept rising until it took its true shape against the distant sky. It was the largest airship anyone had ever seen.

"It must be the size of ten airships put together. How is that possible?" asked Aline.

"They feed their people slop and put everything into building machines of death like that," Sandrell said flatly. "The more reason to stop them and save as many as we can."

Aline could hear the depth of passion in her mother's every word. She hoped Sandrell's rage would not get in the way. Aline also thought it would be good to see her mother in full battle mode again, especially in this place. She smiled at the idea, despite their dangerous mission. Aline stopped smiling when she looked back at the enormous airship. "We may be too late for Artoth, or even Thure."

"We will save those we can."

The massive ship was high in the air now. It looked like a long fat spider in the middle of a large web, with smaller ships surrounding it. It didn't block the light, it seemed to absorb it. The fleet slowly started to move. Sandrell and her waterships waited, hidden, until they saw the entire fleet heading towards Artoth. They scanned their immediate area with spy glasses, but saw no patrols. *Extatumm has more urgent things on their minds today*, thought Sandrell.

"The landing pads are near the coast. The fields are a little farther in. Remember, there will be about twenty guards. I doubt they added any more security since the last report. They needed all of their men for the attack on Artoth. It only takes a few to keep prisoners and slaves obedient and working," Sandrell said darkly, as she gave the final orders before landing.

Two of their waterships went ashore in the secluded spot, while the rest stayed just offshore. Sandrell reasoned that they would need only thirty of their own people to get in and take care of the guards. The problem would be getting out with as many slaves and workers as possible. The hardest part may be convincing some to come with them. She knew that some had worked in the gas fields for so long, they might be afraid to leave.

They could see the guard spires above them, four in all. The tall, slender spires each held one guard at the top of their winding staircases. Taking them would not be hard. The trick was not being seen.

They went along the path, hidden deep in the vegetation that she had used to escape so long ago. They went slow and quiet, sometimes nearly on their hands and knees. They were halfway to the fields when they came to the first guard tent.

It was usually only manned by two men. Since Extatumm normally controlled these waters carefully, they would not expect an attack. These guards were here to keep people in, not out.

They split into three groups. Aline's group went to circle around to spire number one. Another went to the guard complex where most of the guards would be. Sandrell and her group focused on the guard post just ahead. It was a tent like most of the other structures in this part of Extatumm. The canvas walls helped with the heat in this climate. Sandrell wiped her brow, the memories flooding back from the hot, sticky time she spent here.

A scout went forward quietly and peeked under the back wall of the tent. He counted the number of guards and held two fingers up to the rest of the group. Sandrell and three others pulled their short knives and quietly made their way around each side of the guard tent.

The front flaps were opened and they simply rushed in and quietly took care of both guards. They didn't make a sound. Now they had to wait. Each team had to hide by each spire until it was time to change the guard. They always changed the guard towers at the same time. *Big mistake*, thought Sandrell.

The base of each guard spire was far away from each other and hidden by high vegetation. Each team successfully killed their approaching guard, took their key, and entered the bottom of the guard spire. They then walked up the spiral staircase as though they were the regular guard.

Sandrell and her team watched each one in turn. From spire after spire, the signal came that they had been taken. There was only one spire to go and they watched it anxiously. The last spire was taking longer than it should.

They kept watching the opening in the spire tower until they heard a strange noise. It seemed to echo around the camp. Sandrell used her spyglass to look closer at the spire. She saw the hand signal flash out of the opening. All the spires had been taken.

"Spire guard, is all well?" said a man from the ground. He had apparently been eating nearby when he heard the noise. He was wiping his greasy hand on his shirt as he looked up. Sandrell's man stuck his hand out of the opening, signaling to the man on the ground. Sandrell watched as the man on the ground cocked his head to one side and looked to the spire. She was too far away to rush the man.

Just as the man was about to speak again, a small swift shadow came out of the brush. With one hand, the shadow covered the man's mouth, and then they both disappeared into the brush. *That's my girl,* thought Sandrell.

If her calculations were right, there were less than five men guarding the workers now, the rest would be eating. Their timing had been good. It was high sun meal and nearly all the soldiers would be in the same place. Aline and Sandrell gave the signal for the crews to take care of the soldiers in the dining tent. Sandrell and her crew headed to the fields.

* * *

Offshore, the boats waited anxiously. They didn't know how long Sandrell would take. They were constantly watching for the signal to land and receive the workers and slaves. As the main boat commander watched the shore, he was tapped on the shoulder by his second in command. He turned and saw the concerned look. She motioned with her head to look out to sea. Passing nearby was a sentry boat. It was small and only had a crew of three. It almost passed their location when the small ship turned back towards them.

They had put nets out of several of the boats in hopes of looking like a group of fishermen. The sentry boat came closer, and an Extatumm sentry asked, "Do you know something about this spot that I don't?" said the sentry, smiling.

The commander smiled back, "We were hoping to keep our little fishing spot a secret."

The sentry replied, "Not much of a secret," indicating the other boats. Then he cocked his head and noticed that there were two ships parked by the beach. "Friends of yours?" he asked, indicating the ships. "This is a restricted area."

The commander looked innocently over to the boats onshore and said, "No, not friends of ours…"

"Just so I don't get in trouble with my superior, I had better see your…" before the men could finish, there was an arrow in his chest. He fell overboard. The man next to him froze for a moment, but then he started blowing on his whistle and grabbed for his arrow gun.

The crew acted quickly, firing arrows at the sentries. The man stopped blowing his whistle, hit in the chest by two arrows. The sentry ship started to drift with no one alive to steer it. The commander told his men to get on the patrol boat, just as he noticed another patrol boat coming towards them. More whistles sounded the alarm.

Chapter 26

Smoke and Rain

The flames were so intense and the smoke so thick, Brenddel had a hard time seeing his remaining ships. Of the small fleet he brought, only his ship and five others were still in the air. To get away from the ever-widening smoke, he had ordered the ships to break formation and fan out into a rough circle around the large area, scanning for survivors. They were to use their bells if they saw any sign of life besides animals. It had been hours, and he had heard no bells at all. The forest was just burning.

Not for much longer, he thought. Brenddel heard the first drops of rain, followed moments later by heavy tears from the sky. Brenddel wondered if some god was sad that he had burned down the giant trees.

Brenddel felt nothing. It did not seem like Mantuan was dead. He thought he would have some satisfaction; a sense the book was closed. Instead he felt empty as his mind drifted, watching the flames and smoke. He would have to wait until he could search the ruined forest for Mantuan's body, if there was anything left at all.

Asa stood next to Brenddel, also mesmerized by the flames slowly being dowsed by the rain. He thought he should cry for his friend, but the tears would not come. He knew Gordon all his life, and he simply felt nothing. He wondered why, as he watched the flames and smoke, imagining Gordon down there.

Brenddel and Asa watched the wind take the heavy smoke over where the forest used to be, sweeping it down the canyon wall. All he could think about was what he'd been through since he became king. He feared that the coldness from Trunculin, and even Brenddel, was making him lose his ability to feel anything.

Things happened so quickly that it was hard to remember that Gordon had been the king before him. Asa remembered standing there, watching Gordon about to be crowned. It all seemed so long ago.

That was last time he ever saw him. It almost seemed like the Gordon that he knew was different from the Gordon he had been hearing about. Then again, Asa thought, *I'm not the boy I used to be either.* For some reason he thought of his family and how much he missed them.

That's when Asa began to cry.

* * *

Darion was headed to meet the father. As the airship he was given piloted towards the kingdom of the gods he was afraid of what he would see. He knew the plan well, but was still unsure of why it was so important that Extatumm destroy Artoth first.

In his time with the father and his people, he learned much about the way they thought. He understood how much they hated the idea of kings and any kind of faith in a god. He clearly understood their basic philosophy and knew that they would only tolerate his kingship of Thure if he did everything they said.

As Darion's airship came around the last mountain, he could see all the smoke. The father's massive airship was on the island of Asgonan, admiring the destruction. Apparently, the smaller airships and their land army were sufficient to wreak the destruction of Artoth that Darion was now witnessing. The father's massive ship would wait for the bigger battle to come.

Most of the smoke was coming from the areas of the kingdom that housed the two temples. It was hard to get a bearing on exactly where everything was supposed to be, since so little was left. He could glimpse the canal gate off in the distance, and it looked unharmed.

That makes sense, since it was only the kingdom they wanted to destroy.

They were practical enough people to know that they needed to keep the gates working, so that they could take control of the fees for allowing ships through. Darion could barely take his eyes off the destruction of the kingdom, even as his ship was headed to land near the father's large airship. He wondered how much fear the massive airship would instill in his own people.

As his smaller airship came closer, he started to grasp how large the father's massive ship really was. He could see dozens of men scurrying on the deck, manning rows and rows of weapons. He was sure that this airship, alone, could beat any kingdom. He knew he was seeing the future and that he would be a part of it. Darion thought of his dear sister-in-law in Thure. He smiled as he thought of the future, and the look on his enemy's face when they realized just what was really happening.

He kept staring at the ship's skin, which shined like metal, wondering how man could've created such an amazing thing. Darion's ship landed next to TrTorrin's. He was lead to the father, and at first he didn't recognize him. TrTorrin was giving orders to several men around him who held up maps.

The difference was in the way the father stood and the clothing he wore. No longer was he the relaxed, loving father, in charge of the new, kind Extatumm. Now he was dressed as a general, giving orders in a war.

The father turned to him and asked, "What do you think of our work?"

Darion looked at Artoth in flames and replied, "It came down faster than I expected."

The father walked to the railing of the ship and stared at the burning kingdom. "Thousands of years to build on foundations of fantasy and superstition ... brought to ruin in half a day by modern weapons. Isn't it beautiful? The ideas of the past swept away quickly. And forever."

Since Darion was more interested in his own kingdom, he turned to the practical. "Have your ground troops already taken control of the gates?"

TrTorrin replied, "Yes, although one side caused more trouble than the other. It seems the orange warriors have dug in their position. The blue king's army fell quickly and with little resistance. The blue king himself has been captured. The orange king is in the old tunnels. Apparently, it is a vast network under the kingdom. We haven't gotten him yet. Although we burned some of them out of their position near the gate, most of their army is dug in under the kingdom. We haven't found the entrance yet, but I've lost plenty of men trying."

"So, we can still proceed with the attack as planned?" Darion asked.

"Naturally. This was just a small stop on the way. Let's call it practice," said the father. "We should be underway within the hour."

"Good. As planned, I will arrive a good hour after you start your attack on Thure. I've already given you the best targets, the ones that will be least protected. Although, even as they see you coming they will not know what to do. The kingdom has become so fat and lazy that I doubt they mount any defense at all. When you have your fathership over the king's palace, I will come in and save the day."

The father nodded. "And a grateful kingdom will demand their hero be crowned king."

"And when I'm king, the father will come to our kingdom and apologize, beg for forgiveness, and we will sign a peace treaty between our two lands."

"Sparing the civilized world from the godless Extatumm monsters."

"Correction, giving them a peace treaty and therefore introducing Extatumm into the civilized world. Along with lots of trade and coin for both of us."

"Whatever the people need to believe. I have no problem with deception." The father looked directly into Darion's eyes and smiled widely. "As long as you never forget the truth. You work for me."

Darion smiled back, "I understand perfectly."

The father replied, "Let us go win you a kingdom."

Chapter 27

Below

"Is everything loaded?" asked Loren.

Ellice replied, "Yes. Everything is there, and we can leave anytime. Where is Gordon?"

"He wanted to get one more look at the mural. Why don't you go get him? I need to check a few more things before we leave," said Mantuan.

Ellice walked slowly down the stone corridor. She couldn't imagine how this place had been built. The stonework was so massive, and it was built thousands of years ago. Everything must have been done by hand, but each block was so precisely cut that it looked like it was made by machine.

As she passed the intricately carved shapes in the rock above the archway, she also looked downward, noticing how large the blocks were that supported the walls. "How did they even get the stone here?" she whispered to herself.

When Gordon was first shown the underground city, he almost did not want to leave. He had endless questions for Mantuan. Every question reminded Ellice of his father, whose mind was always so full of questions.

They had been so young when they married. It was only the beginning of his fifth trial, after being cheered on by the people to take the second set of trials. They said at the time that he was the most loved king in a hundred years. They were young, in love, and everything was right. She thought that Daymer had forgotten all about her. They had met when they were just children, but then he was king and she was still just a poor village girl he had once known.

She remembered how he had begged her not to look at him differently, how he had only been chosen king at random. He had nothing to do with it, he said. He insisted he was still the same boy, just a little older, and that the crown meant nothing. He always said that once the 'king business' was done they could go back and live a quiet life.

How wrong everything had gone.

But that didn't matter now. The suffering was over, and now she was rewarded with the son she thought she had lost so long ago. The future was bright again.

The long arched corridor opened up abruptly into the massive room. Ellice smiled as she looked around the large stone walls. Gordon's back was to her, and he was mesmerized by the large mural painted on the wall.

"I wish we could take that with us," said Ellice.

Gordon looked around and smiled, then looked back to the painting. "Why do you think they did it, mother?"

Warmth rolled through her as she heard the word mother. "I don't know, son. We don't know anything about these people. No one knows how they built this place, or for what purpose. Why do you like the painting so much?"

"I don't know," replied Gordon. "You see how it starts over here? The people are farming and playing. They seem happy. In this middle part, there are two sides fighting. And over here there are children outside of the battle. It's not clear if this soldier is protecting them, or if they're an enemy."

"Does it remind you of yourself? Of a more innocent time, before things went wrong?" asked Ellice.

"I don't think so," Gordon struggled to articulate his thought. "Look at this part towards the end. It looks like things are different, but also the same. There's is a king there, with his crown. I don't know. I guess it just reminds me of everything."

Ellice replied, "Go on, I want to understand what you're thinking."

"These people probably lived thousands of years ago, and they were going through the same things that we're going through now. Fighting and kings and people trying to live their lives. It just seems like we keep doing the same things over and over again. It feels like things never really change. I don't know how to explain it."

"I think I understand. It feels like we are going in circles forever."

"Yes. That's it."

"And this painting makes it seem like the world has always been the same. There is an endless circle of men declaring themselves king, and war, and suffering. Like it will never end."

"Yes," Gordon replied.

"I understand. Mostly, that's true. Man seems to make the same mistakes over and over again. But there were a few men and women that found a way to break the circle. You don't know how great our kingdom once was. You may have read a few threads of real history, but so many other truths have been buried. Not just by Trunculin, but men like him that didn't want to believe there was an answer, a way to live that was unlike anything before."

"You mean the first thirteen kings?"

"I mean the first thirteen. But actually, only four were kings."

"What? I thought ..."

"I know, most people assume the kingdom of the thirteen means that there were thirteen kings. But it doesn't. When the first thirteen came to the land that would eventually be our kingdom, none of them were kings or queen. Many left their lands because their rulers were monsters. Only four became kings, and one was a queen. The rest were brilliant men and women who helped set up our system of kingdom."

"Like the triangle idea? So that no one side is greater than the other?"

"Yes. In other lands, kings have say over everything, even life and death. The first thirteen believed it best to have three corners - one with the king, and the other two with equal councils. Important matters had to be agreed on by all three to be a law."

"Then why do they call it a lower council and an upper council if they're equal?"

"They used to be called the corner councils. They are supposed to be equal. Over time, it was changed to make one council seem less important. Calling it the lower council is an insult."

"So, this is what you've been guarding and collecting all these years? Proof about the way our kingdom was supposed to run?"

"Yes. That, and so much more. I have true histories written at the time when the history was being made. I'll admit, I was angry when I heard about how you were made king. Making someone king goes against all of the ideas of the first thirteen, whether it was Trunculin or Mantuan who arranged it. But now, I'm beginning to think having someone that Trunculin did not choose is the only way to restore our kingdom."

Gordon replied, "That sounds impossible. If Trunculin has changed things that much ..."

"I know. I thought that for a long time. But your father didn't think so. He felt things were wrong somehow, like you do. He didn't have the tools to fix it. I have those tools. But it will not be easy. I almost gave up, thinking it impossible too. But we are both here, alive, so anything is possible. Now that I have you back, I don't want to see you in any danger. But there is still danger ahead for the whole world if Mantuan's plan doesn't work."

"Mother?" Gordon asked.

"Yes, Gordon, my son? I really like saying that."

"Me too." Gordon asked quietly, "Do you ... do you think my father would have been proud of me? I mean, I'm only thirteen. I haven't done that much. Mostly I've been rescued and helped..."

Ellice pulled him tight in an embrace. "Your father would be bursting with pride." She looked into his eyes. "I know whatever distant shadowy lands he's in, he's proud of you. And I'm proud of you."

"I'm sorry to break apart a mother and her son, but it's time to go," said Mantuan as he approached.

"Of course," replied Ellice.

"Mantuan, how thick are these walls, anyway?" Gordon asked as they all moved back towards the ship, down the long stone arched hallway.

"Uggh, more questions. Very curious, our king. We think the walls and ceiling are ten feet thick, solid stone. No fire could touch us here. No matter how intense it gets. Whoever they were, they built it to last," said Mantuan.

"To think that the real fortress is hidden deep below the trees," remarked Ellice.

"A forest of three hundred foot distractions. I am sorry to see those trees go. Some think that they were as old as one thousand years. Aline will probably never forgive me. But it served many purposes for the forest to burn. The burnt forest will seal the entrances forever. We may be the some of the last people to see these rooms." Mantuan said, "Still, the forest is a terrible loss. But we live, and I will see that the forest is re-planted after this business is over. Our distant ancestors will haunt the forest again."

They made their way to the largest part of the ancient underground fortress where the airship waited. The enormous room had no pillars and could have held another airship the same size. No one could explain how the ceiling was supported. The fact that it was there to protect them was all that mattered.

"Ready to leave all this behind?" asked Ellice.

"Yes, it's time to set the world right. Our home is in the kingdom of the first thirteen. It's time to take our place there," said Mantuan.

"Or die trying," added Gordon.

"The three of us have been dead before. Wait until Trunculin sees us alive and together," Ellice smiled.

"If only a great artist could capture the look on his face," added Gordon.

"Seriously Gordon, the road we take now still holds the most danger for you. Your sweetblood illness is under control now, but you could go out of balance anytime. No one would blame you for letting others fight this fight. Are you sure you're ready?" asked Ellice.

"Yes mother, I'm sure. If this path will help restore the kingdom and clear your name, I'm ready. And I don't want to be 'Gordon that has the sweetblood.' I just want to be Gordon."

"Well said, *just* Gordon. Let's get to it then," said Mantuan as they boarded the ship. Mantuan saluted the corner of the room and the ship maneuvered carefully through the cavern that went from finished stone to rough cave wall as they exited far down the cliff face. They paused at the exit of the cave and surveyed the area. They saw no air ships coming, but it was hard to see anything in the smoke and rain. As Mantuan had planned, the thick smoke from the fire on top of the cliff wall would hide their escape.

They piloted the airship under the thick smoke and used it as a shield as they left the canyon. Soon they were miles away, imagining Brenddel's army sifting through the forest, looking for bodies they would never find. Mantuan hoped Brenddel understood what he had meant when he spoke of truths and smoke.

Chapter 28

The Battle of Thure

The Extatumm fleet made their way towards Thure. The crew on board the ships kept careful watch of the waters. They would be flying nearly the entire way over the dark seas. The waters began to roil with the finned Jhalgon fish, but none broke the surface for more than a moment.

They seemed to be scared of the massive fathership. TrTorrin noted with satisfaction. "Even nature fears us," he said aloud to his crew. But he knew the truth. His thinkers were able to do much with the body of the Jhalgon he'd killed. They knew the rotators attracted them, now they knew how to repel them. The sound being emitted from his airships was silent to men, but the Jhalgon heard. So far, they stayed in the waters.

The fishing vessels, both large and small, gave a wide berth to the incoming fleet and the giant fins directly underneath the airships. The world had never seen such a large collection of airships in one place, and no one had ever seen an airship as large as the fathership. At 803 feet long, it was not easy to miss at any distance.

The father surveyed the massive, sprawling kingdom of Thure. It stretched from its large main port, all the way along the massive landmass. The various cities ran right into each other inside the walls of Thure.

The fleet made a strange sight as it flew towards the kingdom. The sun was at the back of the fleet so that they all appeared as large black objects in the sky from the kingdom of Thure. The father smiled as he imagined the fear his fleet must be causing.

Below them, the waters were still swarming with life. It looked like a large boiling carpet had been laid out below them. Every airship had done maneuvers over open waters and knew how to take the creatures down. The arrow men kept watch, their weapons pointed straight down at the waters the entire flight. But the fin creatures did not attack, the new silent devices working well.

With information from Darion, the targets had been chosen carefully. The idea was not to destroy anything near the palace, where many people lived. That would cause a future alliance nearly impossible. This mission was much subtler. A large show of force attacking sites that were inhabited only by the poor. None of the rich or connected would be directly affected by the attacks.

That way, when Darion, the future king, flew his 'stolen' airship out of the sun to rescue the kingdom, the rich and powerful would still be alive to demand his kingship. King Darion would also be able to visit the poor areas affected by the attacks and build the love of the people.

The idea that one airship could send the fleet back to Extatumm was ridiculous, of course. But heroes had been made on thinner deceptions. The plan would work and it would have the correct effect on many of the people with influence in the old kingdom of Thure.

The father reflected on his real plan of disrupting the ancient bloodlines. It would be an historic insult to the royal bloodline that led back to the Queen of Dard. *She is going to hate that her granddaughter will no longer be queen*, thought TrTorrin. The father liked the idea of taking care of several problems with one blow.

Once Darion was fully installed as king, it could go several different ways. One, the king would be the best person to make peace with Extatumm. Only a king that had publicly defeated them could make peace with an enemy. Or two, the kingdom of Thure could hold this attack against them forever and never make a public alliance. The second way would work just as well, since King Darion would be secretly working for Extatumm. If the king decided later that he didn't need the support of Extatumm, the father had two courses. He could either use the proof that Darion was in league with them, or he could simply bring back his fleet and destroy the kingdom for good.

There was no way to lose.

The father quietly smiled to himself as the fleet neared the kingdom. He wondered to himself if Darion really understood the weak position he was in. The father looked down at the waters and could see the beasts swarming beneath them.

He also saw all the ships that worked out of the port of Thure. They almost looked like they were lining up like a column of soldiers, saluting their vast airships. The boats stared at a site the world had never seen, thought the father proudly. There were more ships than he expected. He imagined a mixture of fear and awe on the waterships as they watched the great attack. The father intended to put on a very good show. They would not be disappointed.

The older commanders were glad that this attack was just for show, since they understood how hard a real fight would be. They knew better than anyone how difficult it was to remove ancient bloodlines. They also remembered how often they had come close to defeat in the old days of Dard.

Many of the younger commanders had been upset at the plan. They were true believers in the new world, and they wanted to destroy any semblance of the old. They wanted the attack to be real, but the father had cooled their blood and explained that they were playing a much longer game.

The father gave the orders to begin. The fathership stayed over the waters while half of the ships neared their attack points in different parts of the kingdom. The weather was perfect. The father gave the order and the airships let their great arrows fly at the old kingdom of Thure.

Chapter 29

The Gashouse

Sandrell and her crew had no idea what was happening just off the coast. They had secured the dining tent, all four guard spires, and were now headed towards the fields. They were nearing the entrance when they heard the whistles coming from the coast.

Sandrell knew that sound well. Years ago, when they realized she had escaped, that noise echoed everywhere. From the brush, she had to crawl through to the cold dark waters. The whistles rang in her ears. She heard the guard boats circle until she was sure she would be caught. Even when the whistling stopped that night, and she was safely away, she heard them sometimes in her dreams.

These whistles were no dream, and she sent four of her crew to go stop the sound. Unfortunately, some of the guards of the fields had already heard the noise and were running towards them.

Just as the men were about to pass, Aline came out of the brush and swung her longknife across their path as they were running. The blade took them both in the chest. They were no longer a threat. The whistles had finally stopped, as they scanned the area for more guards. *There should only be three or four more.* Sandrell wondered if ... but she put that thought away. Surely Fortistaf was dead, or attacking Artoth with the others. She tried not to think of the man who used to be in charge of the guards. She never found out why he was sent here, but she knew what he was capable of. That kind of man wanted to practice his cruelty where the rest of the world could not see. *But that was years ago. Concentrate.* She focused on the task at hand.

Sandrell knew that there were no whips for the slaves. The guards were all chosen for their large size, cruelty, or both. Most of the time that was enough, but when any alarm was sounded, they also had plenty of weapons. The guards would all have their knives drawn, waiting for them. The element of surprise was gone.

Sandrell gave the signal to split into two teams and to circle around the long buildings where the workers and slaves lived. Her team found two more guards. They apparently thought it was a drill and hadn't drawn their longknives. They were casually chatting and unconcerned until they saw strangers come upon them.

They were taken care of quickly.

Then they saw their first worker, a young girl carrying water. Some of them worked outside the fields assisting the soldiers with various tasks, others worked inside the gashouse building. Sandrell saw that the girl must be going back towards the gashouse. She looked surprised and dropped her water as Sandrell put her finger over her lips and whispered to the girl. She told the girl why she was there. The girl's eyes lit up with surprise and hope. She nodded that she understood. A team went with the girl, walking quickly to tell the other workers and slaves.

They had secured the guards' area and the spires. Another team was securing the workers' quarters. The whistles had stopped. All that was left was the gashouse. It was a long rectangle building where the lifting gas was produced. The kingdom of the thirteen used a lifting gas that came out of the ground, separated and stored. Extatumm has discovered how to make a lifting gas. They called it water gas and it was made in the gas production building. Some guard had called it the gashouse and everyone working at the gas fields now used the short name. The so-called gas fields were actually abandoned mines and open pits where Extatumm had looked for their own naturally occurring gas and precious metals. They never found gold or any of their own lifting gas. But they still called them the gas fields. *Even the names that Extatumm uses are lies*, thought Sandrell.

Sandrell had listened very carefully in the time she was a prisoner here. The men who made the gas had started with acids and metals to produce the gas. Over the years they found better ways to make the gas from water, while using complex machines to make and store the gas. There was only one problem with the gas Extatumm made: It tended to explode. Unlike the sun gas from the ground in the kingdom of the thirteen, the gas Extatumm produced was highly flammable. There had been lots of accidents in the early days, one of the main reasons the gashouse was so far from the capital.

The water gas was just a little lighter than sun gas, and since they made it, instead of finding it, larger ships could be filled with the gas. They could build a fleet of any size. But TrTorrin had a hidden weakness. Since this was the only gashouse in Extatumm, Sandrell would take away the father's ability to build new airships.

Sandrell and Aline were outside the building, where there was just one door. They opened the door quietly. A guard had been waiting for them inside and swung his longknife. He overextended his reach and Sandrell simply pulled him over. He tumbled to the ground, and Aline used her shortknife. The guard wouldn't attack anyone ever again.

Only one or two guards left, Sandrell thought. Aline and her mother stood inside the door. They had their weapons drawn, but no one ran at them. They both tried to pierce the gloominess of the long building. The large machines in the middle hummed loudly. There was a large boiler at the center, with pipes and a complex system of valves and tubes. The noises could mask footsteps, so they kept a close watch.

The door opened behind them. The same little girl stood there. She put her finger to her lips and led Sandrell outside, leaving Aline inside to guard the door.

Outside stood the rest of Sandrell's team with the workers and slaves. There were more than three hundred. Sandrell took a breath and said to those gathered, "We've come to release you. We have many waterships waiting to take you out of this filthy place. Is this everyone?"

A woman who looked very much like the girl said, "This is all of us."

"Any more guards?" asked Sandrell.

One of Sandrell's team said, "There were two more we took down. This woman says there are only two more in the gas building."

"We got one already," said Sandrell.

The woman stepped forward. "You are the one that escaped, aren't you? They still talk of you in whispers."

Sandrell responded, "Yes. Now we will all get out of this evil place." She looked at the woman, "When I was here, there was a very large man ..."

The woman nodded, looking into Sandrell's eyes. "Fortistaf. He is still here. He was inside the gas house."

Sandrell's blood froze. She said, "Get them to the ships, now!" as she ran back to save Aline from a monster.

Chapter 30

Letters

Brenddel continued to watch the forest burn. The fire was nearly out. Only smoke remained, thanks to the torrents of rain. The wind blew the fading smoke away from them and down the cliff face. But they still had found no one. Brenddel could not shake the feeling that something was wrong.

Where were the bodies?

Brenddel has lost many airships and men thanks to Mantuan's tricks, but it almost seemed too easy. As though the young king was reading Brenddel's thoughts, Asa said, "Why didn't they put up more of a fight?"

"I was just thinking the same thing," replied Brenddel.

"I expected this legendary warrior Mantuan to never give up, to fight to the death. But he just seems to have given up and died."

Asa asked, "And where is the airship they stole?"

"We surrounded the forest. It was too dense for the airship to be hidden inside. The cliff was too steep to escape by climbing down. I guess they hid the ship somewhere else. That's possible. But if they're going to make their final stand here - who would be left to collect it? They hid airships underground in Extatumm, but they couldn't do that here. There is nowhere to hide, nowhere to escape to." said Brenddel, as he watched the smoldering fire.

His eyes followed the trail of smoke down over the cliff. What had Mantuan said? 'Follow the smoke?' 'Smoke and truth?' He thought it strange at the time. *What did the old man mean?*

Brenddel said, "I hope you will indulge me, my king, but I want to check out the canyon. Maybe the cliff wall will give us a few more ideas. Maybe they were foolish enough to climb down with ropes after all. Seems ridiculous, but I have a strange feeling."

The king agreed and they took one of the smaller airships. The large ship, *Justice*, was well equipped for many things, but not for maneuvering near steep canyons. They made it around the smoldering forest and down the canyon as he ordered his remaining crews to recover any of their own soldier's bodies that they could.

They descended as quickly as possible and were facing the steep cliffs. Its rocky surface was jagged with multicolored stone. Brenddel was not someone who cared about rocks, but the king couldn't help but remark how interesting the different colors and patterns were. Brenddel could see no signs that people had been there. No ropes hung there. No sign of climbing.

Brenddel didn't know what he was looking for. Maybe a metal ring that been inserted into the stone to hold the rope for the airship? He did not see one. He did spot a few holes that looked to be small caves or shafts, but they were barely big enough for a man to fit through and certainly couldn't hide an army.

He looked down to the canyon floor and couldn't believe what he saw. Men were down there, wearing his soldier's uniforms. They were not moving. He wondered if Mantuan had dragged his men over the cliff. He thought, *I might have done that, but it doesn't seem like Mantuan's style.*

They were facing the canyon wall, and Brenddel's eyes began scanning again for some pattern in the random works of nature.

The king said, "Look at that," making a line with his finger. He had his head turned to one side as though he was seeing something new.

"There?" asked Brenddel.

"No, there," once again pointing and tracing his finger along a strange looking line.

Brenddel also cocked his head to one side and could see that the line was odd from this angle. He told the pilot to fly to the left. As he did, the line changed and became what looked like the opening to a large cave.

Brenddel and the king looked at each other, and he told the pilot to go farther to the left until they saw that it was clearly a very jagged opening in the cliff wall. He told the pilot to get closer. As they did, they realized it was a strange illusion of the eye. If you looked at it from a slightly different angle, it became an entirely different thing. It was clearly an opening. But they could not tell if it was a shallow opening, or something deeper.

"Let's take the ship in. It looks big enough," said the king abruptly.

Brenddel looked at the opening warily and replied, "I don't think we should risk an airship just for curiosity. Jagged rock can cut an airship open just as easily as a knife."

"It looks big enough to me. I just learned 'history is not made by timid men.' I forget who said it."

A shadow of a smile came over Brenddel's face. "Borenn, our first king did. Who am I to argue with that?" He ordered the pilot to take the ship slowly into the large opening.

The pilot obeyed orders, but Brenddel could tell that he was not confident of the decision. The airship made its way into the cave very carefully, maneuvering the changing angles of the cave walls. After a few moments, it was clear that this cave was very deep. As they slowly made their way in, the rough cave walls gave way to an enormous space.

It was made of stone, clearly cut by man. The walls were decorated with all kinds of symbols and shapes. It was large enough for several airships. There were no pillars supporting the ceiling.

"How did they build this?" asked the king.

"I don't know. Clearly this has been here a long time," Brenddel answered.

The king ordered the ship to spin in a circle, so that they could take in the spectacle of the great room. They could only guess what it had been built for. It was clear that it easily survived the fire far above it.

"Mmmfft!" echoed through the great room.

"Look!" said King Asa.

In a corner of the great room, the soldiers that Brenddel had sent into the forest were tied and gagged, "Mmmfft!" said one soldier through his gag.

Brenddel ordered the ship to land. The soldiers were untied and they told their stories. A few of the soldiers were missing, the ones at the bottom of the cliff. There must have been tunnel traps that shot the men out of the cliff walls. Brenddel wondered, *why did Mantuan spare the rest?* But was glad he lost less soldiers than he'd thought.

There was now no doubt how Mantuan's army had escaped, and why they let the forest burn so easily without a fight. They had been hiding in these great rooms the entire time.

The lead soldier from the forest said, "They left something for you."

Brenddel replied, "What?"

"It's over there."

Placed carefully against a far wall were two letters. One letter was addressed to Asa, and the other was addressed to Brenddel.

Gordon wrote Asa's letter.

Brenddel's letter was written by Mantuan. His letter started with, 'Don't tear up this letter…' and ended with '…and bring my axe.'

Chapter 31

Under Attack

The first wave of attacks had begun.

The first airship concentrated on the small marketplace about a mile outside of the palace city. It catered to the poor and the servants of the rich. No fire was to be used, but a volley of large arrows made an effective attack.

The second ship attacked a neighborhood of three-story buildings. There were shops along the bottom, and the upper two floors housed regular Thurians. This target was chosen because there was an obscure series of statues in the courtyard there that would serve as a symbolic attack on the kingdom itself.

It was an effective attack. The statues all toppled over, and the area was in ruins. The third ship was to attack a small dock. It was known as the dock of the sorrows, since it was always last in line to catch anything in the bay. Mostly small family fisherman used it, and all the boats were working out in the waters. They used rock guns on the two small buildings and the dock. The buildings flew apart into splinters. In reality, it was a harmless but symbolic target, one that attacked some form of shipping business in Thure.

Darion and the father had chosen the targets carefully so they would have some impact, but would appear random. No one should be able to guess that they had detailed maps of the kingdom. That would complicate things later, if someone started to ask questions about Darion.

The three ships withdrew after the attacks. *Time for the next step*, thought TrTorrin. The father had been watching each attack with his long spyglass. He noticed that the areas were emptier than he expected. The father considered this, but didn't think it all that strange since it was in the middle of the day and people were bound to be drawn out of their houses to wherever they worked.

The second wave was to be five separate targets. Two of them were closer to the palace city this time, but equally as harmless with only a small loss of life. As the airships approached their new targets, the men manning the weapons began to take aim and make their measurements for a decisive line of fire.

Then something unexpected happened. Out of nowhere at each of these targets, it appeared that everyday citizens were assembling into action. Large weapons appeared. The people pulled large blankets off of very large arrow weapons. There were also giant launchers to hurl stones.

Before the commanders could make sense of what they were seeing, these weapons opened fire on the airships. Lines of arrow men appeared on top of Thurian rooftops and walls. They took very accurate aim at the airships.

The large arrows fired from all directions at each of the airships. It was as though the attack was coordinated, as though they knew where the attacks would be. TrTorrin's men tried to get their bearings, but before any of the large weapons on board the airships could be fired, all of his airships near Thure were under attack.

They didn't seem to be firing at the men on the decks, but instead they were firing at the airship's gas chambers themselves. Two ships fell from the sky almost immediately, while another was losing air quickly and fell into the sea. Shadow fins immediately attacked the crew and fallen airships. The silent sound devices kept them from attacking, but did not help when their meals came to them.

There was no point in trying to rescue those men. Another ship dropped from the sky inside the walls of Thure. Another airship was clearly damaged and fell from the sky outside the kingdom walls near the ruined dock. It suddenly caught flame and went up like it was made of dry paper.

A large arrow pierced the deck of the fathership. TrTorrin looked over the edge. The boats and ships below them were all opening fire on his airships. A large stone hit a smaller airship nearby, spilling men off the deck.

The father stared at the counter attack with amazement and anger. Something was very wrong. *They were ready for us.* There is no way the lazy kingdom of Thure could organize this quickly, he thought.

Out of the great port, he saw Thurian ships. At the head was a large warship. On deck, the grandmother shouted orders, "Concentrate on the big one. That's where the father will be!" The former queen of Dard had all of her weapons aimed at the fathership.

Before he could ponder the possibilities any further, all of his airships were under attack. More of the mighty stone was being hurled at them from different weapons over the kingdom walls, many hitting their targets. More airships fell.

The fathership was too far out at sea to be a target from Thure's main weapons. The waterships were mostly using small arrows. He knew he would have to take action or much of his fleet might be lost. He had obviously been betrayed. He just hoped they didn't throw fire at him. He hoped to have at least one secret left.

Chapter 32

Small Cut

"Little one. No one is here to rescue you," Sandrell heard as she flung the door open to the gashouse. Aline was facing her, with her longknife out, circling a man. The man had no shirt. His heavily inked back was to Sandrell. He was holding a short fighting staff.

He sniffed the air.

"No, it could not be ..." said the man, "... can it be my fierce little bird comes back to me?"

Sandrell stood motionless.

The man turned around to her. "It is. My little bird, you have flown back."

He started walking slowly towards her. Sandrell stared, but did not move.

The man asked, "Where have you been, little bird? I have missed you."

He kept approaching. Sandrell had her long and shortknives ready.

He stopped and took notice of Aline again. "Ah, is she a gift for me? For running away so long ago? I forgive you. Let me give you a kiss," and he opened his mouth. His teeth were sharpened into fangs, just like the men of the orange king in Artoth.

Sandrell did not speak, but Aline noticed that she was in a fighting stance, ready for anything.

"Hmmm, she looks like your … no, could this be a daughter? My new little pet bird will sing for me at night. Maybe she won't peck as hard as you."

"Aline, get out," said Sandrell.

Aline did not answer, but flew at the man instead. He was ready and countered her slashing knives. His staff blocked both blades, and the man connected his weapon with Aline's shoulder. She yelled and launched at him again. This time she cut his arm.

He looked at the thin line of blood forming on his arm. "Oooh, I like her," he said to Sandrell.

Sandrell and Aline were side-by-side now and the man had his back to the door. The young worker girl rushed in. "They are almost to the beach …" the girl froze when she saw the bare back of Fortistaf. He turned to her quickly and bent down. "Let's play little one."

Fortistaf grabbed the little girl. The girl was too afraid to scream. He began running to the back of the building with the girl flung over his shoulder.

Sandrell said, "I'll get the girl. You find the hose that pumps the gas out of the building."

"You know what it looks like. I'll get the girl," said Aline.

"No time. I've described it in detail. You know what to do. Don't argue."

"But…"

"*I* must kill Fortistaf," her mother said as she ran after him.

Aline watched her run after the man and the little girl. She reluctantly went to look for the hose assembly.

The girl finally screamed as Sandrell raced after them. It echoed through the building. The gashouse was big, with lots of places to hide. The girl stopped screaming. Sandrell thought, *I only hope it's because he covered her mouth.*

Sandrell got to the back wall of the building. He was there, and he was not trying to hide. He had only wanted to separate mother and daughter. The little girl was behind him, heaped on the floor and afraid to move.

Fortistaf launched at Sandrell, swinging his short wooden staff. She blocked each move easily, despite his huge size and massive arms.

"I always liked the fight in you, little bird," he said.

Sandrell answered, "But now I have weapons to kill you. Or are you going to talk me to death, Fortistaf?" as she swung her longknife at his head.

He blocked the blow as Aline came up quietly behind him and put her own body between the man and the little girl.

Aline whispered something to the girl. Then, with no warning, Aline launched at the man with her long and shortknives. He blocked her blows with his short staff. As they fought, the girl followed Aline's instructions and ran past them.

Sandrell yelled, "Keep going, and don't stop until you get to the beach!"

Aline positioned herself close to Sandrell. The man took a step back and looked at them both. "When I have beaten you both, I know a place deep in the mines to keep you all to myself." He pulled at the center of his staff. It slid apart to reveal two blades hidden inside. He looked at his twin short knives and launched at Sandrell.

The man cut his knives through the air, and just before they hit Sandrell, she bent over, impossibly low to the ground to avoid the blow. She pushed her longknife deep into the belly of the man. The attacking rage on Fortistaf's face changed to one of surprise. Sandrell withdrew the long blade as he fell. He groaned and stopped moving.

Sandrell spat on the man and turned her back to him. They both ran for the exit.

Sandrell asked, "You unhooked the hose?"

"Yes, the gas is already filling the room," replied Aline.

"Good. We need to get out fast. The gas has no odor, and it will fill the building quickly."

By the time they reached the exit, some members of her team had come back with rope and oil. One team was on the beach, securing the slaves and assisting them onto ships, while laying the rope and pouring the oil onto it.

"How far does the rope have to go?" asked Aline.

"All the way to the beach. Be generous with the oil so that the rope catches fire quickly," said Sandrell.

"It will be a pleasure to see it burn, especially knowing that the monster's body will burn with it," said Aline.

"These fields are going to do a lot more than burn," said Sandrell. They finished laying the oil-covered rope, and the rest of them went to the boats, leaving Aline and Sandrell.

Sandrell stood, where she had been a prisoner. "No one will ever be a slave here again." Sandrell looked around.

"Is anything wrong?" asked Aline.

Sandrell replied, "No, Aline, I will just be glad when this place no longer exists."

Aline nodded and unwound the last part of the rope. She was just sliding it under the door of the gas building when she was knocked over. The impact of Fortistaf bursting through the door sent her to the ground.

He had wrapped some dirty rags around his wound, but they were solid red already.

Aline rolled away from him and got to her feet. She drew her knives and backed away. She was sure he was mortally wounded. Fortistaf staggered backwards clumsily.

He held only one staff blade in his hand. Fortistaf held his wound with the other. He staggered backwards and kicked the rope away from the building.

Sandrell walked up to him. He was too slow to avoid the attack. She slashed the arm holding his wound and he growled.

Aline started to attack. Sandrell screamed, "No! I will kill him."

Aline stood with knives in hand. She went back to the rope and put it inside the door of the gashouse again.

As Sandrell was walking towards him, Fortistaf smiled and looked at Aline. He made one final lunge at Aline, but Sandrell was already there.

He turned on Sandrell instead and slashed at her with his knife. She tried to avoid it, but he was still surprisingly fast. She was cut along the forearm, and she had no time to assess the wound. It didn't feel too deep. Just a small cut.

He staggered again. "Why do you make me hurt you, little … little bird?"

Sandrell watched him. "You've lost a lot of blood, Fortistaf," as she got between Fortistaf and Aline.

He blinked and made another weak jab at her, but Sandrell knocked the staff blade from his hand. She kicked at his leg, and he went flat on his back. More blood gushed from his wound. He didn't try to get up again.

Sandrell put her blade away and poured more oil on the rope. Her vision was a little blurry. She shouldn't be fighting in this kind of heat. *I forgot how hot it gets here.* Aline kept her knives out, watching over Fortistaf, who was only a few feet away. He was too weak to get up from the sand.

"My… my little bird," the man said, breathing heavily. "When you left I had to do a few things differently to make sure no one else got away. Do you feel it yet?"

She ignored the man, and was still struggling with the rope. But she was sweating, and the sweat was getting in her eyes. She looked at her wound. *I was right, it's only a shallow wound.* She noticed tiny bubbles in the wound. She looked at Fortistaf, who tried to laugh. "It is a very dangerous fish. The poison is very fast."

Fortistaf was on his back, but he raised his head. Aline looked to her mother. Sandrell blinked furiously, wiping at her wound. A yell rose and Aline was flying. Her feet landed on either side of Fortistaf.

Her blades landed in Fortistaf's chest.

Sandrell staggered and blinked harder, trying to clear her vision. Aline went to her mother. "He's lying, mother."

Her mother blinked and shook her head.

"No! This can't be happening. He was lying about the poison." She saw her mother's wound, but it didn't look serious.

She knew it was.

Aline searched her pockets frantically, but she knew it was no use. She had no zoress bread with her to draw out the poison. Loren had it, and he was half a world away.

Sandrell staggered to her knees. Aline said, "We'll get you to a healer."

Sandrell replied, "We are oceans away from any help. I can feel the poison working, daughter."

"Don't you call me that! You only call me that when things are bad. You'll be fine. I won't let you go!"

"Aline. Aline, my brave daughter, I need you to do something that will be very difficult."

"No!" yelled Aline.

Sandrell put her hand on Aline's face. "Look at me, daughter. You have to let me go," she said calmly. "I will stay behind and light the rope. I have to do this and you have to let me go. At least I will be the last one to die here."

Aline couldn't process what she was hearing. "No. No, mother. You can't leave me. Don't leave me."

"I am so sorry I couldn't be there for you. After I escaped, I thought I was cursed. You were safer with Mantuan. I'm sorry I stayed away … I wish I could change things, but … I will always be with you. I love you, Aline."

"Don't say that!"

"I know you got your stubbornness from me, but do this last thing for your mother. Take my knives and tell great tales of me."

Aline was crying. "No…." and she suddenly wiped her tears away, decision made. "NO! We will set the rope on fire from the beach. You will not die in this place."

"Aline…"

"No, mother. Get up. You will not die next to that monster."

She helped her mother to her feet. Sandrell was too weak to argue, but somehow she stood and Aline almost had to carry her to the beach. As soon as the crew saw them, they rushed to help Aline and her mother.

Aline touched her forehead to Sandrell's. They stared into each other's eyes, but all Sandrell could do was nod her head.

Aline made sure Sandrell used the last of her strength to light the rope on fire with her own hand. Then Sandrell closed her eyes forever. Aline carried her to the boat and they launched in silence.

The boats were a few hundred feet out to sea when the ground shook. Everyone nearly went deaf from the massive explosion. To Aline, it looked like the flames rose a thousand feet into the air.

She imagined her mother riding the flames to the gods.

Chapter 33

The Fathership

The father felt a wave of nausea hit his stomach. The air seemed to vibrate for a moment. He sensed it had nothing to do with the battle somehow. He turned his mind back to reality. As though they were reading his deepest fear, the weapons from Thure suddenly unleashed fire arrows.

The father shouted, "Give the signal to pull back."

As he gave the order, he finally saw Darion's airship coming into view. Darion's ship came alongside the fathership just as all of the fleet was regrouping around the massive ship.

Darion shouted, "The queen seems to be more resourceful than I expected."

"She seemed to know exactly where we were going to attack. Quite the coincidence," answered the father.

"No coincidence. I told her exactly where you were going to attack. She's been preparing for this attack for weeks," answered Darion.

The father's face turned into a mask of fury. He screamed, "Arrow men at the ready!" Before the father's arrow men were in position to fire, Darion's arrow men were already aiming at the soldiers on the fathership. TrTorrin saw his own men on Darion's airship tied up. The men aiming at the father were Darion's soldiers.

"I just wanted to stop by and let you know who it was that defeated you," said Darion. "Did you really think I would be in league with the people who want to see the death of all kings? I just wanted to give you a moment to pray to whatever gods you used to believe in, before the fire burns you out of the sky. You should have kept your secret deal with Trunculin for their gas. Their gas is not as flammable. Terrible flaw, you know. Oh, and by now another team will have already blown up your gas fields."

The father was trying to figure out if Darion was lying. "You're in one of my ships filled with the same gas," said the father. "Before my ship goes down, I'll make sure that yours does as well."

"I think my friends will have something to say about that," Darion said, pointing at the airships approaching from the rear. "Looks like Mantuan's army has found your missing airships."

Mantuan's airship came into view with the five stolen Extatumm airships.

The father took a small arrow gun from one of his men and fired. It missed Darion and struck the guard beside him. Darion's men fired at the Extatumm soldiers and soon all the men were firing at each other.

Just then, a large fire arrow flew from Mantuan's ship. It went directly into one of the smaller airships at the rear of the fathership. The airship burst into flame and fell from the sky in seconds. The father watched as the five Extatumm airships and Mantuan's own ship surrounded him.

The large Thurian warship was nearby and hit another airship with a large fire arrow. It exploded. On board the grandmother cheered with her men.

More of TrTorrin's airships were hit. The father stared in fury, as Darion's airship started to float up and away.

Since all of the father's ships were so close together, Mantuan did not need to hit each ship with fire arrows. The fire on one ship caught to another, as embers from another ship caught the next.

Airships were falling from the sky all around. The smaller ships were all busy trying to get away from the growing catastrophe.

Darion's airship was floating just outside of the cluster of ships, maneuvering upward to avoid any fire. The father told his crew to concentrate all arrows big and small at Darion's ship, which was still in range and just above the fathership.

Several large arrows hit Darion's ship and it immediately began to lose height. The deck was no longer level and Darion found himself falling over the balcony of his own ship.

Darion fell, his body twisting in the air, until he landed on top of the fathership. Several other men fell with Darion. Two of the men hit the top of the fathership. One man kept rolling, and fell to the waters below. Darion and the last soldier found ropes and held tight to the top of the ship. They watched their own ship fall from the sky.

Darion and his soldier looked around for any way off the fathership. All they saw were other ships bursting into flame and falling out of the sky. Mantuan's ship was close by, but they couldn't even signal without losing their grip on the ropes.

Mantuan's ship came closer, probably looking for the best spot to destroy the ship. Darion was hoping that they had been seen. As he turned his head to follow the progress of Mantuan's ship, he saw that someone was pulling his soldier off his ropes. His soldier screamed as he lost his grip and was thrown to the dark waters below. TrTorrin had climbed up the rope ladder attached to the ship. He was on top of the fathership now, standing with sheer force of will, coming slowly towards Darion across the ship.

On board Mantuan's ship, Gordon watched the father making his way towards Darion. Mantuan's ship was hovering twenty feet above them, looking for the best shot. No one saw Darion except Gordon. Knowing how important a secret ally Darion had been, he had to do something.

Most of the men on board were engaged in shooting other ships. Gordon looked around and saw the he was the only person not doing anything. He quickly tied a rope around his waist and tucked another rope inside his belt. *Mother is not going to like this*, he thought. Gordon took a breath before he did something he knew he would regret.

Mantuan saw him at the last moment. Ellice saw him too and shouted, "Gordon, no!" But it was too late. Gordon leaped from the railing. It was closer than he thought, and he landed just next to Darion, hanging onto the same rope he was. The father was getting closer, going as fast as he dared, now that he had two targets to throw off his ship.

TrTorrin was enraged and walked faster, despite the danger of falling. Gordon took the second rope and was trying to tie it around Darion's waist. The two men used their free hands to work together.

They had just barely finished tying the rope around Darion's waist just as the father was upon them. Darion was quickly pulled off of the fathership and was safely out of TrTorrin's grasp.

The father was upon Gordon, still boldly standing upright on the airship. He pulled Gordon by the rope around his waist until he was standing right in front of him. "You stupid boy. I should have killed you."

Mantuan and his crew were tugging on Gordon's rope, but the father used his rage and held it firm. He screamed at Gordon, "You kings will die away, one by one. We are the future, and we will never stop."

Gordon tried to tug on his own rope, but the father held it tight, making sure that he could not be pulled up. By now Mantuan, Ellice, and two other men were pulling on Gordon's rope. But the father still held the rope firm, clutched Gordon by his shirt, and said, "If I die today, boy, so do you."

Gordon started to shake.

"What are you doing?" asked the father.

Gordon breathed hard and desperately reached for his belt.

TrTorrin laughed. "What? Is this your sickness? A weak, sick boy plucked from the filthy mob to be king? Your kingdoms will all die, just like you will from your sickness, boy." TrTorrin grabbed Gordon's throat and squeezed with his left hand.

Gordon used his right hand to feel for his belt. Gasping for air, Gordon found what he was looking for and jammed it into the father's belly. He looked at Gordon's shortknife, letting go of the rope. TrTorrin's hand released the boy's throat.

Gordon said, "Whatever kills me, it won't be today."

He was quickly pulled off the fathership and back to Mantuan's ship as the father held his stomach, and pulled out the knife. He threw it to the waters below. TrTorrin, the father of Extatumm looked up. Mantuan's ship was directly above the fathership.

The last thing the father saw was a column of fire pouring down.

As Mantuan's ship gained height, the fathership exploded in midair. The remains sank immediately into the swirling, finned Jhalgon creatures below. They would be feasting on Extatumm meat all day. The only airships left in the sky were Mantuan's small fleet of ships. The enemies from Extatumm were totally destroyed.

The victors made their way to the palace of Thure.

Chapter 34

Feast

They landed at Thure and were greeted with heroes' welcome. The next few days were a time of peace. Both sadness and hope arrived a few days later with Aline. The ships were all unloaded, and the slaves and workers were all received as heroes. Aline would only speak to Mantuan. The queen of Thure had a funeral pyre built for Sandrell. Aline lit it herself and had been alone in her chamber ever since.

After a full day's rest, there was a public feast, where all cheered for the heroes of the Battle of Thure. Afterwards, the queen invited them all to a private chamber where they could talk.

Gordon asked, "So, all of those waterships had your men onboard?"

Darion replied, "Yes. The queen and I had been in constant but secret contact, planning to defeat TrTorrin. My men in Aspora hired every ship they could find. I had already pledged my army to the queen's cause in secret."

The grandmother said, "I'm just sorry my warship didn't fire the shot that killed TrTorrin."

The queen replied, "At least you helped in his downfall."

The grandmother said. "Thank you for that. Your grandfather was with me in spirit on that ship. We got rid of the monster, but they still hold my lands in Dard."

"Taking Dard back will have to wait for another day," said Darion. "If we asked, I think the two kings in Artoth might help us with that.

And with the five airships that Mantuan has given us, we have more tools now."

"I'm sure Artoth would help. I have already told the queen, but my brother Santovan reports that the war is going well in Artoth," said Denogg. "The blue king was rescued by the orange king himself. Santovan says it's a hopeful sign that they worked together to retake their kingdom. He said the destruction is terrible, but the two kings will work together to rebuild. The nasty Extatumm army has retreated back behind the Gates of Dard. They don't seem to know what to do without their father."

Mantuan asked, "Is it true that you got your house back?"

The queen interjected. "It is true. After all of the adventures, it is clear who the real enemies were. I can't bring my husband back, but it would be unfair to keep Denogg's fortune."

"In fact, we have already begun talking about how we can be partners in some business," added Denogg. "I have many ideas. With this new beginning, maybe I can help improve the fortunes of my own kingdom, instead of just helping yours."

"It would be nice to have some wealth to go along with all the paper," said Darion.

The room laughed, but soon grew reflective.

"To lost friends," toasted Loren. They all drank.

"How is she?" asked Gordon.

Mantuan said, "Aline will be alright, in time. Sandrell is a terrible loss."

Lantovas, the Firstman of Thure said, "You might just ask her yourself." He stepped aside, and Aline was standing there.

"Mind if I join you?" asked Aline.

Mantuan rushed to hug her.

"Please pardon me, my queen, but she asked to join you all," said Lantovas. "I hope I did not overstep my authority."

"Of course not," replied the queen. "After all you've been through, you should join us as well. It is not every day that the Firstman of

Thure helps in the battle to save our kingdom. Mantuan tells me you manned the fire weapon that destroyed TrTorrin's ship."

"I did my part. Thank you, my queen, I would be honored to join you all." Lantovas came into the room and joined the group.

Mantuan finally let Aline go. "I'm glad you came."

"Thank you Manny." And she quietly went to a chair between Gordon and Mantuan.

Gordon stood quietly. Soon, they were all standing. He didn't say anything, just raised his glass and looked at Aline. They all did. Aline nodded her thanks and wiped away a tear. Gordon noticed she was wearing her mother's longknife.

"Alright, enough," said Aline. "I'm sick of crying. I thought this was a party."

They all laughed gently and Lantovas said, "I'm just glad there are no creatures around to attack me." Everyone in the room laughed harder.

"Queen Ellice, it has been too long since we have welcomed another queen here in Thure, besides my grandmother, of course," said the queen of Thure. "How are you feeling?"

"Stuffed with joy," said Ellice. "The world is a brighter place. I have my son and my brother returned to me. Thank you all for what you've done."

"To new beginnings," Mantuan said, raising his glass again. They toasted. "Not to spoil the party, but there is still important work ahead. The immediate threat has been stopped, but the true villain must still be destroyed."

"And that is my signal to retire to bed," said the Grandmother.

Mantuan replied, "My apologies. We can discuss other matters."

"No, but thank you," said the grandmother. "The new world you are all helping to create will take some getting used to. I am old and slow to change. I leave these battles for the young," she said, kissing the check of her granddaughter as she left. They all stood as she exited.

When the Grandmother was gone, Darion said, "She is a great lady."

"Yes," The queen replied, "and she is also right. These battles are for others. Even my role is nearly done, for now. King Gordon, when Trunculin is removed from his power, your kingdom will have the support of Thure."

"Thank you, my queen. We'll need it. Until then, what's our next step?" Gordon asked.

Mantuan replied, "Queen Ellice has been taking care of the former slaves and workers from Extatumm. We still have to clear your mother's good name, restore Gordon's crown, and prove Trunculin's lies. We must do all of this while not getting killed by Brenddel and his army. Word that Gordon and Ellice are alive will already be spreading throughout our kingdom. Trunculin will try to convince the people that they are all lies. I have people working from inside our kingdom. They will spread the truth."

Loren added, "History has just been written in front of the eyes of our entire world. Even Trunculin can't control that. But we still have to be very careful how we go forward."

After much debate, they finally decided on a plan. After it had been laid out in detail, Denogg said, "You are all crazy people. I am in the wrong business. I should write this all down in a book. I'd make a fortune. Of course, no one would believe it."

They all laughed again and made their final plans.

Chapter 35

King Asa's Decision

"You should have done this sooner," said Brenddel as he looked out on the unruly crowds. "They want someone's blood now."

"I would gladly give them Gordon's, if he were here. Too bad you didn't bring him back," replied Trunculin, surveying the crowds that had gathered.

"I have heard the whispers. Some think Gordon may have been wronged somehow. Some are calling him the hero of the Battle over Thure," said Brenddel. "The pamphlets that you had circulated among the people, some say they are lies. They say the rumors trickling in from the old kingdom are the truth."

Trunculin exploded. "And it's your job to make sure the people are in line!"

Brenddel said, "My duty is to protect the king and the kingdom. Don't blame me if the crowds don't believe your lies anymore."

Trunculin was furious, but also a little unsettled. Brenddel had never spoken to him like that before. *What was wrong with him lately?* Thought Trunculin, "Yes. Well ... let's get this over with. Will you tell the king it's time? Please."

Brenddel nodded courteously and went to get the king. Trunculin went over the speech in his head. He was walking the finest line he had for his many years. The news out of Thure was bad, very bad. Not only had Mantuan and Gordon become heroes, but they had utterly destroyed Trunculin's secret ally. Extatumm launching two sudden attacks on other kingdoms made them look like monsters, confirming everyone's worse fears.

Trunculin looked guilty of siding with a madmen.

Blaming the alliance on the new king would be easy, but making villains of Mantuan and Gordon would be difficult. Push too hard in his speech, and the crowd would turn away from Trunculin. But he thought he had found a way to reach all his goals in one speech. He smiled to himself as the king approached. Trunculin thought King Asa looked bored.

"You understand how to proceed?" Trunculin asked the king again.

"Yes, yes. I start and then say that you can speak my mind better than I could. Then you start your speech," said the king.

"Correct. Shall we go?"

They walked out into the center of the courtyard and the crowds applauded politely. There were no cheers. Several councilors were there as representatives of the two councils. Trunculin made sure that they were councilors firmly loyal to him. Trunculin shouted to the crowds. "Your chosen King Asa wishes to say a few words about recent events."

The king spoke to the crowds. "Honored citizens of the kingdom. Thank you for coming. As I am still learning to be the best king I can be, I have asked my Firstcouncilor Trunculin to speak on my behalf."

The crowds gave thin applause. Trunculin began. "Thank you, my king. As many of you have heard, there was an attack on the kingdoms of Artoth and Thure by the traitors from the far lands of Extatumm."

There were loud shouts from the crowd. *Not a good beginning*, thought Trunculin.

He continued, "Our king wishes me to apologize on his behalf for his mis-judgment of the near alliance with those people. He now realizes the error of his ways and is glad that the enemy was defeated."

A loud roar of cheers erupted from the crowd.

"You have also heard that some former soldiers were responsible for the victory. These are lies. The people that defeated the traitors were the Queen of Thure and the brother of the dead king in Thure.

But also, our own Firstman Brenddel and our King Asa helped in the battle. They were on the very airship that took down the father's ship."

There was some cheers but mostly there was confusion among the crowds. *That's a very bold lie*, thought Brenddel.

Trunculin dramatically motioned towards the king and Brenddel standing beside him. "Yes, these brave men helped defend the old kingdom of Thure, our true ally."

Asa stood there uncomfortably, shifting his weight. *The crowds will never believe that*, he thought.

Louder cheering was heard. Trunculin motioned for quiet.

"As in many great battles, there are always fanciful rumors and lies floating about. I have heard rumors that the slaver queen is alive. The very queen that brought so much shame on this kingdom a generation ago, and the queen that was married to the king that took his own life, jumping off an airship to his death. And I have just confirmed that this rumor is, well … true."

The audience gasped.

Trunculin smiled to himself. He had the audience with him again. "She is alive. And I say that the shame of the past should stay far away from us …"

"Firstcouncilor! If these things are true…" said the king, coming towards Trunculin. He abruptly turns to the crowds and said "… people of the kingdom, if this is true, doesn't the law demands a trial?" Asa then turned to the firstcouncilor expectantly.

Trunculin fought the urge to stab the king and hurl him from the stage. Instead he said, "My… my king, the past cannot be undone. Why bring that slaver woman back into our kingdom even for one moment?"

Asa nodded reluctantly.

Trunculin thought to himself, *well, whatever that was, it's over.*

Then Asa turned dramatically to the crowds and said, "For justice! Why should we let these people escape the justice of our kingdom? Isn't there a law that we must try these people? That they must answer for their crimes?"

The crowds went wild at the idea.

Trunculin looked to his councilors for support. The two were furiously looking through some papers. "Councilors," said Asa. "Doesn't the law state that serious charges, such as these, must be answered?"

The councilors looked at each other and looked to Trunculin for what they should do. Trunculin glared at the councilors. The two looked through their stacks of papers again, as the king said, "Well, councilors? Should there be a trial?"

Finally, one of the men looked up and said, "My king…," said the councilor nervously, looking to Trunculin and then back to the king. "That is what the law says." After that, the councilors only looked down, not looking at the firstcouncilor again.

Trunculin was doing his best to keep his composure, but he could feel it draining away. He was feeling a little lightheaded after this quick turn of events. The king gave him no rest as he continued, "They must be brought to trial quickly. I believe all citizens should view this trial. It must be an open trial for everyone to see, so that there is no injustice done behind closed doors."

The crowd's cheering could not be contained. It went on and on as Trunculin narrowed his eyes and looked back at the councilors. They did not look back at Trunculin. He looked around the large crowds and felt only white-hot anger.

"The people have spoken! Let the trial be in three days! Justice will be done!" King Asa briskly walked off the stage followed by Brenddel, who gave a hard stare at Trunculin. The rest followed clumsily, including Trunculin.

The king went back to his quarters and Trunculin was there within moments. Brenddel and a small group of soldiers assigned to the king were all there. Trunculin came up to Brenddel and said as calmly as he could, "I will see the boy now."

"The king will not see anyone right now. Firstcouncilor, we need to speak." Brenddel said, as he walked out of the room and Trunculin followed. They were in a quiet place where they could talk openly.

Trunculin nearly spit out the words. "What was that? What is that damned boy doing?"

"We grew closer on the trip to bring down Mantuan. He told me everything and he is very angry with you. Did you really have my soldiers do that to him?" asked Brenddel calmly.

"The boy … he had to understand the way things really work. It was only a few times and I left no scars. I think he got the message," replied Trunculin.

"And now he's trying to embarrass you. Gordon and Mantuan cannot come back to this kingdom. Neither can the queen. We both know why. The king trusts me now. I can soothe his temper over, but you need to work on your councilors and find some obscure law to stop this. He's just told the whole kingdom there will be a trial in three days. That *cannot* happen," finished Brenddel.

Trunculin reasoned. "That will not be easy. Both counsels defied me with the treaty, and they are much harder to control these days. It's too late to have *nothing* happen in three days. The people need some kind of trial to satisfy them. I can supply the proof against Queen Ellice, Gordon, and Loren. But none of them can show up for this trial. We can try them in absence, find them guilty, and pass sentence. That will satisfy the crowds."

"Good. And I will make sure that no one gets into the kingdom. I will lock down the docks and set a blockade by air."

Trunculin pointed at Brenddel. "That will work. It has to work. And it's your job in the future to keep that boy on a leash."

Brenddel replied, "Yes, firstcouncilor. I agree."

Trunculin walked off. Brenddel made sure Asa's guards wouldn't let Trunculin see the king. Then he went to the docks. The note placed on his trophy wall was something only he would notice. No one ever touched his prizes. He followed the instructions and went to the small ship. In case it was a trap, he told his best man to lock down the docks if they didn't hear from him in one hour.

When he went below on the small ship, he was surprised to see the mystic there. He was more surprised to see the other man. They told him quite an interesting story. Brenddel walked away just under an hour later, knowing exactly what he had to do next.

Chapter 36

Battle of Gray Mists

Word of the trial came quickly to Thure. Gordon and Mantuan made plans to go, but they knew how risky it was. The odds were that Brenddel would take them prisoner and they would quietly disappear. The recent word they got from their kingdom was hopeful, but Brenddel was still the biggest problem. If they didn't show up for the trial, it would certainly prove they were cowards to the entire kingdom. Ellice was convinced they would not get a fair trial as long as Trunculin had any influence, even in public. She did not accompany them back on the airship.

Mantuan felt that it was better to go at night, in order to bypass any sentry ships. There was much discussion whether daylight would offer more protection, since they couldn't be taken prisoner in front of witnesses. It was hard to hide an airship in the daytime sky. Mantuan assured them that he had a plan, and the cover of night was best.

There was a seldom-used docking station for airships. It wasn't too far from the palace, next to a set of buildings that were used only for storage, no guards or soldiers.

Mantuan piloted the ship himself, and they kept the crew small. Only Aline, Gordon, Loren, and two other men were aboard. They floated to the kingdom and arrived in the middle of the night. The thick gray mists that settled over the kingdom aided them. It would be harder to see them, even with their lanterns lit.

They approached carefully, constantly scanning for other airships. It was a very foggy night, which offered them cover, but also made it nearly impossible to see other airships approaching. They were nearly to the station when Gordon thought he saw movement in the sky close to them. "Look! There …"

But no one else saw anything. They were not stopped, so Mantuan hoped his information was still good about the docking station. He was surprised he remembered where it was, especially in the heavy fog. If they docked and were met by an enemy, it would be too late to escape. Mantuan hoped his gamble worked.

"Where are we exactly?" asked Gordon.

Mantuan replied, "The docking station and storage buildings are built on the side of the mountains just outside the palace city. See there?"

Gordon could just make out the structures through the gray misty fog. There were wooden walkways built like a large square. One side of the square was missing so that an airship could float between two sides of the square. There were two open-ended squares next to each other, so two spots for airships. They would be docking to the platforms over open air, secured to the two sides with no ground underneath.

It reminded Gordon of a watership dock, where you could put the boat in between two walkways on either side and get out. This was for airships, though, so it was huge. And unlike watership docks, there was no water to fall into if you tripped. The airship just floated in between the two walkways over nothing but air.

"How do we get off if we don't actually land on solid ground?" asked Loren.

Mantuan replied, "There are bridges that raise up from the sides. It locks in place to our deck and we simply walk over the boards. Don't worry, it's safe." One of the men took a long pole from the railing and hooked the hinged bridge. It swung up and he attached it to their deck.

"Good idea," said Gordon.

"Yeah, if you don't fall," replied Aline.

They had docked and were tying their ropes off so that the airship wouldn't go anywhere. That's when they heard the rotators of another ship. Mantuan saw the airship and headed for the connected dock next to theirs. He knew who was on the airship. He could feel Brenddel staring at him through the fog. The ship moved closer and they could see that the ship had their weapons aimed.

Brenddel called out. "There is nowhere to go, Mantuan. Abandon your ship."

Mantuan looked to Gordon, then called to Brenddel. "I will meet you half way."

The hinged ramps were brought up and connected to each deck for Brenddel's ship. There was now over a hundred feet of ramps connecting the docked ships. Brenddel's men kept their weapons aimed.

Brenddel walked to the center of the platforms. Mantuan did the same. They stood facing each other as Gordon, Loren, and Aline followed cautiously behind Mantuan. No words were spoken as the men came face to face. Brenddel and Mantuan did not draw their longknives, but they both kept their hands on the hilts of their blades.

"Brenddel. I wasn't sure if you'd come."

Mantuan offered his hand.

Brenddel took Mantuan's hand slowly. Both men relaxed their stance. "I'm still not sure I'm convinced of everything, but many things in the letter make sense. Your main agent showed me more proof. However, some of what the mystic told me, I'm not so sure ..."

"It's all true," said Mantuan.

Brenddel shook his head. "And your main agent ... I had no idea you reached that far into the palace, right under my nose. I just hope you have the rest of the proof you say you do. Oh, I brought you something."

It was wrapped in cloth. Mantuan smiled and opened it to reveal his battle-hardened axe. "I thought I would only see this again if you were attacking me with it," said Mantuan.

"Not long ago, I was planning to bury that in your head," replied Brenddel.

Mantuan nodded. "I'm glad that time is over. And don't worry. We have proof of everything. We even have a witness that was told to keep your mother alive at all costs until Trunculin made you find her."

"I knew he was capable of horrors, but I never suspected he could … the things than man asked me to do. He turned me into a monster. I let him. I've been trying to kill the wrong man all this time," Brenddel said.

"If I had been in your place, I might've thought the same thing. Trunculin's greatest power is his deception. He fooled us all at one time or another," replied Mantuan.

Brenddel looked at Gordon. "I'm sorry I tried to kill you."

"Thanks," said Gordon, "I'm glad you didn't succeed. So, what happens now?"

Brenddel answered, "Now, we quietly get you into the kingdom and hide you all until the trial tomorrow. Last I checked, the firstcouncilor had the forged documents to prove your guilt. But he will not be able to stop the people from showing up. And he will not be able to stop you from speaking."

"That's good." Gordon said, but he seemed distracted.

"Is everything alright, Gordon?" asked Mantuan.

"Everything's fine. It's great. It's just that … it's just that all this time, I thought my vision, or dream actually meant something. But in my vision, I was falling from an airship, and you two were fighting. I don't think you two are about to fight each other, are you?"

Brenddel replied, "That's in the past. I wish … " but instead of finishing his sentence, Brenddel drew his longknife. Mantuan sensed something was wrong too and spun around with axe in hand. The mists were still very thick. They could only see a few feet in front of them.

Then Aline and Gordon heard the rotators.

Suddenly, a volley of small arrows came out of the fog from the airship just coming into view. An arrow came so close to Gordon's face, that he felt the wind from it on his cheek. Everyone got down lower.

But it was too late for Loren, who took an arrow. Gordon saw the arrow go in, but he didn't hear Loren make a sound. Another volley of arrows came through the fog. As the ship floated closer, Gordon could see the flame coming. He shouted, "Fire!"

They all scattered just in time. The fire hit the wooden walkway and it erupted in flames. Gordon, Aline, and Loren ran back to their own ship's deck for cover. Mantuan and Brenddel ran to Brenddel's ship. Brenddel's men were firing their weapons at the large ship. Brenddel knew it was their large new ship the Justice. *And I have a good idea who's aboard.*

Two men from the Justice were roping down, firing arrows at Brenddel's ship.

"They are men still loyal to Trunculin. I guess he doesn't trust me anymore."

Mantuan replied, "Let's go kill them, son."

Brenddel came around the other side of his deck and jumped onto the rope, firing a wrist arrow as he did. The man on the rope was hit and fell, disappearing into the fog below. Brenddel climbed the rope to the deck of the large ship. Mantuan slung his axe onto his back and followed up the rope.

Next to Mantuan's ship, the man on the rope was dangling only a few feet from them, trying to see them through the fog. Aline turned to Gordon and Loren. "Stay here," as she leapt onto the rope. The man on the rope was startled by the attack and even more surprised when Aline's smallknife went into his belly. He dropped from the rope. She climbed the rope to the deck of the large ship.

Gordon stayed with Loren. The arrow was sticking out of his uncle's arm. "I'll be fine Gordon. Stay here until they get back."

"But, I have to help," said Gordon. But he suddenly felt dizzy. The thirst hit him like a wave. *No, not now*, he thought. Gordon shook his head, fighting the sweetblood attack.

"Gordon, are you having a reaction?" asked Loren.

Gordon nearly growled. "I'm fine." He regretted talking to Loren that way. *But why now?* He had no time for a sweetblood attack. He was so tired of having one more problem added to his life. Why him? It wasn't fair. He looked at Loren with the arrow sticking out of his arm. Gordon had no idea why the gods gave him this illness, but he decided it would not stop him. Not today and not ever. He wasn't going to stand by while more people got hurt. "I'm sorry, but I have to go. I'll be back soon."

Loren began to protest, but Gordon was already off the deck. He steadied himself and blinked through the fog. Gordon shook his head and looked for a rope to climb to the large airship. He ignored the thirst and the dizziness.

Gordon finally climbed to the top of the rope and saw men fighting on deck. The fog was very thick, and he could only see a few feet in front of him. He heard the clanging of metal and the shouts of fighting. He smelled the metallic tinge of blood. No one had seen him, so he climbed on deck and drew his longknife.

He scanned the deck for Aline, and then he heard, "Gordon, look out!" as a man came flying at him out of the fog. Gordon raised his blade just as the man impaled himself on it. The man dropped his own knife, but the momentum of his body pushed Gordon to the edge of the railing. He pulled his knife out, but hit the back of his hand on the railing, dropping his knife. He heard it clang on the deck. The continuing momentum of the large man pushed them both over the railing.

Gordon was falling.

The vision came to him. Instead of a world on fire, the world was a haze before him. Everything seemed to be going very slow as he tumbled backwards. The wind rushed past his ears. He saw the fire below. The wooden walkway was still ablaze, but obscured by the thick gray mists.

No! I won't die like this. Time to save myself. Gordon blindly reached out, not knowing which way was up. His finger brushed the rope and he grabbed wildly. Just when he thought he was lost, his fingers wrapped around the rope. He stopped abruptly, but held firm, and his arm protested the strange angle. His muscles ached, and his palm burned from the rope. This was no vision. He wrapped the rope around his hand to make sure he was secure. He closed his eyes and willed the dizziness to stop.

He dangled there and lifted his head up and opened his eyes. Over the railing, he saw Mantuan, Aline, and Brenddel all pulling on his rope. His hand burned, but he held the rope tight until they finally pulled him back on deck.

Aline said, "That was close, my king," and she hugged him tight.

Gordon said, "Yes, I … I think you're right."

"Was this like your vision?"

He hugged her back, "More like a dream."

She let him go with a smile.

Brenddel asked, "Are you alright, my king?"

Gordon replied, "I never thought I'd hear you call me that again. Did you get them all?"

"They're all dead," said Mantuan. "We will get a man up here from my ship to pilot the … what did you call it?"

"The Justice," answered Brenddel.

"That's a good name. Who were they?" asked Gordon.

"They used to be my men," said Brenddel. "Several of them were put on Kings Asa's guard by Trunculin while I was gone. They did some nasty things for Trunculin. I was going to punish them for what they did. I don't have to anymore."

"We need to get Loren to a healer. And … I don't … feel very well," said Gordon, breathing heavily, fighting his thirst.

"We'll go right now. I know a healer that has no love for Trunculin. She will help us and keep you hidden until tomorrow," Brenddel said.

Mantuan smiled and said, "That's my boy."

* * *

Only an hour after the attack in the sky, the watership came out of the fog and into the harbor. It docked on a quiet, older dock just out of the main shipping lane.

The hooded figure that came to meet the ship was glad the fog was so thick. There was no moon for him to be seen by, but the fog diffused the moonlight so he could still make his way over the dock. His meeting with Corinn and Brenddel had gone well. The mystic Valren was safely tucked away until he was needed. *Only one last task before tomorrow.*

A small group of people got off the ship. As he approached them, he lowered his hood, "Queen Ellice?"

The queen extended her hand and said, "Thank you for meeting me. I have been told nothing but good things about you."

"And I you, my queen," he replied.

"I doubt that, but thank you for saying so. After tomorrow the history will be corrected." Her traveling companions were still coming off the ship.

"And until then, Queen Ellice, I have someplace safe for you all to stay."

"I've heard you've been very busy putting everything in place. I look forward to hearing what you have planned. Lead on, King Stathen."

Chapter 37

Begin the Trial

Trunculin had not slept. He had gone to meet with the mystic earlier in the morning so that he would be fresh for the damned trial.

But he didn't feel any better after the session.

Since yesterday, the palace grounds had filled with more citizens than Trunculin had ever seen. There was no way to stop people from coming, but he had been working for the last three days to turn the trial to his advantage.

The little king still wouldn't see him, and Asa was still surrounded by Brenddel's closest men. He deeply regretted not killing the boy when he had the chance, but he couldn't go back and do it now. He had tried to bring Asa's family to his interrogation rooms, but Brenddel reported that the family had moved away. They were just gone, he said. This news did not help Trunculin's mood. He had no leverage over the brat king now.

The airship that he had sent to make sure that Brenddel was still loyal, had not been heard from. It was only a gut feeling that Trunculin had about Brenddel. He almost felt bad suspecting him. But now that the ship he sent to follow Brenddel is missing, he felt more uneasy. He could find none of the men from the airship that were loyal to him. He feared the worst for them, and he now assumed the worst of Brenddel. Trunculin couldn't just ask Brenddel to look into the matter.

He thought it odd that King Asa had named that ship Justice, and that 'justice' could not be found. He hoped that was not a strange message from fate before the trial.

The Firstcouncilor personally checked with all of the councilors that were loyal to him. All of them were firmly against the trial, but none of them moved to do anything about it. *All useless.* Trunculin began to realize how weak his hold really was without Brenddel's help. He had several conversations the last few days with Brenddel. The firstman had said all the right things, but Trunculin couldn't help but feel that he was just going through the motions. He couldn't tell Brenddel he had sent an airship to spy on him, and Brenddel said all of the airships were accounted for.

He still hoped he was wrong about Brenddel.

Since Trunculin had lived such a long time in service to the kingdom, he knew how dangerous paranoia could be. But he couldn't help it. Suddenly, everyone did seem like they were out to get him.

At least none of the witnesses had shown up. Brenddel had kept his end of that bargain, at least. He said there were no attempts, but he wondered if Mantuan had tried to come in, and perhaps Brenddel had killed him quietly. He would have to look for a patch on Brenddel's trophy wall. That thought gave him warmth as he walked to the courtyard to begin the trial.

As firstcouncilor, he would serve as the representative of the kingdom. He had all the evidence that he needed to convince everyone that his version of history was correct. He had been very careful over the years about making sure his lies became fact. At least as far as the records were concerned. He held in his hands many forgeries, but no one need know the truth.

Trunculin walked out with all the papers in his arms. As he came out into the sunny day, the size of the crowd was staggering. *Is the entire kingdom here?* He thought. For such a large crowd, there was only tepid applause as the firstcouncilor strode out dramatically.

Since it was outside, people were standing around him on all sides. It felt like he was on a stage once again. Trunculin knew that he would have to give the performance of his life. On one side was every member of the two councils, and to the other were a series of empty chairs. The witnesses and people on trial would have been seated in those chairs.

In the middle, on a raised platform, was the king's chair.

It was customary for the king to be the judge in large trials, especially concerning traitors to the kingdom. Because he had not been able to tell the king what he was supposed to say, Trunculin knew that the king was the most dangerous unknown factor in this situation.

Trunculin had sent several notes to the king, but he had no idea if he received them. The most important note told him the fact that the king was to choose someone of importance, usually another councilor, to defend the prisoners.

Of course, since no prisoners would show up, this 'trial' would be over quickly, and Trunculin knew that. It made no difference which counselor the king chose.

It had been so long since Trunculin had allowed any sort of large trial that he had to refresh himself with the law he had helped write. The last such trial had been to condemn the slaver king and queen. Since one had died and the other had fled, it was over quickly. The entire crowd agreed with Trunculin that they should be struck from the history books all those years ago.

The king and Brenddel walked out, and the crowds erupted in applause. Trunculin noted with annoyance that it was the kind of applause he used to receive. They walked in front of Trunculin. The king sat in his chair with his heavy judge's staff. Brenddel stood beside him as firstman.

The trial had begun.

"My king, have you chosen my opposite?" asked Trunculin.

"Yes firstcouncilor. I have chosen King Stathen," replied King Asa.

Trunculin was surprised. *That's an odd choice*, but Trunculin and never had any serious problems with King Stathen in his ten trials. He was an unruly boy at first, but they all were. Former King Stathen walked out onto the stage and nodded politely to Trunculin. He took his place at one of the small, high tables that was there for each of them.

Trunculin began, "My king, fellow citizens ..."

"My king," Stathen said, interrupting Trunculin. "I know it is customary for the prosecutor to start. First, I would like to have all of the people involved take their seats."

"My king," said the firstcouncilor. "That is not the law. Which people do you refer to?"

Stathen said, "These people." And on cue, a line of people came out and took their seats.

The firstcouncilor watched in horror as Gordon, Mantuan, Queen Ellice, Loren, and several others walked onto the stage and took their seats.

Trunculin stared at Brenddel, who stared back and nodded his head slightly. *I have lost Brenddel.*

"My king," said Trunculin. "Former King Stathen has invited traitors to the stage, even the slaver queen herself. I ask that these traitors be removed from the site of these good citizens so that none of the lies can burn in their ears."

The crowds did not like this and shouted their disapproval. They were ready for a drama.

King Asa thumped his staff on the platform, and simply said, "They will stay. They will speak."

Trunculin thought furiously the best way to turn this to his advantage. "Very well, my king. It doesn't matter, since I have proof that they are all traitors to you and our good people. Allow me to tell the people who these traitors are. We have the slaver queen here, whose husband and herself brought slavery to our kingdom. And here, we have the former firstman of that very king. He helped hide all the evil the king and queen were doing," Trunculin continued walking down the line, pointing to each person.

He was careful not to walk too close.

"And here we have a former firsthealer of the kingdom, who helped a scared little boy run from his duty of being your king. He also hid that the boy has the sweetblood illness, which makes him unfit to be king. We even have the young sick King Gordon himself. I say every person on the stage has betrayed our kingdom," Trunculin finally finished.

Stathen said, "And I will show, my king and great people of this kingdom, that every single person on the stage is innocent. The lies told about them and their downfall all came at the hands of one man, the Firstcouncilor Trunculin."

Trunculin laughed. "Oh I see. The oldest trick of the truly guilty ... blame their crimes on the innocent. And not just an innocent man, but a man that has served faithfully with everyone on this stage. I was the one that was betrayed by all of their evil. And it was I who had to clean up all of their messes. Former King Stathen makes it sound as though I was the one on trial."

Stathen said, "Your lies reveal the truth..." He turned to Trunculin. "You are the one on trial, Firstcouncilor Trunculin."

Chapter 38

The Trial Turns

The massive crowd made an audible gasp of surprise. Trunculin looked around at the king and the councilors, and then back to Stathen. He was not smiling. "What is the meaning of what you just said?" Trunculin asked carefully.

Stathen turned to Trunculin. "I mean exactly what I say. You are the one on trial this day, for crimes against the kingdom. You are not the prosecutor here. I am. And you are free to ask for someone to defend you."

The king tapped his staff, "Firstcouncilor Trunculin, who do you wish to name as your defender?"

Trunculin looked around and wondered how he had gotten to this place, on this day. He thought about being indignant and simply walking off the stage, but he would only look guilty. He also noticed that there were guards posted at any place he might exit.

Trunculin said proudly, "I need no defender besides myself. I have nothing to hide. But be warned, my former King Stathen, I will not stand here and be found guilty by rumors and lies. You will need solid proof. Since I have done nothing wrong, there is no proof to be had."

"I have all the proof I require, and I will show it today. These good people will know the truth," replied Stathen.

Stathen noticed many of the councilors looked very nervous. He knew there was no gracious way for them to leave. "Let's start with your more recent crimes. Isn't it true that you had members of the king's guard beat our new King Asa on several occasions?"

The crowds gasped.

"An outrageous lie. I never touched the king! I know nothing about our new king being hurt. If some soldiers had hurt the king, I hope that he would have told me. I would have had the guards locked away," said Trunculin, boldly looking at King Asa.

Stathen asked, "My king, I know it is not customary for a sitting king to give testimony, but since you were directly involved, did Trunculin order the beatings?"

The king spoke. "Yes. Several times when I was in the old kingdom of Thure, he had four guards beat me. He watched and smiled. It only stopped when my Firstman Brenddel returned and posted his most trusted men as my guards."

"My king, you have put me in an impossible situation," said Trunculin. "I am your humble servant and could not possibly suggest that you are not telling the truth. So how am I to defend myself? Could we ... could we all see these bruises? If what you say is true, you must have terrible bruises from such beatings."

"It was a while ago. All of my bruises have healed."

Stathen replied, "Don't worry, firstcouncilor, there is proof of this. But first I would like to point out another crime that happened only recently. Last night, soldiers from this kingdom, under your orders, attacked the airship escorting some of these witnesses. In fact, all four of the men that beat the good king were on that ship. These men shot Loren with an arrow. You can see the healing cloth there around his arm. Brenddel also witnessed these attacks. Do you deny this action?"

"Yes, I deny. How would I order soldiers to do anything? The firstman of our kingdom is in charge of the soldiers. They take orders from him. Where are these men?" asked Trunculin.

Stathen answered, "Unfortunately, in the ensuing battle all aboard were killed."

"How very convenient."

"All but one. He nearly died, but was revived by a healer. He is well enough to speak now. Bring him out please," said Stathen.

Trunculin was nervous. He bribed those men because they were strong and stupid. If they were faced with prison, he had no doubt that they would talk. They brought one of the guards from the ship, walking slowly with a limp. The Firsthealer Corinn helped him on stage. She looked right into Trunculin's eyes, and a cold chill went through him.

"Soldier, were you ordered to follow, and even attack Brenddel and Mantuan's ships last night. Is that true?" asked Stathen. "And did the firstcouncilor order you to beat the king on several occasions?"

The soldier looked at Trunculin and back to Stathen, "Yes. It's all true. The firstcouncilor ordered me to do those things."

Stathen asked, "My king, is this one of the men that beat you under Trunculin's orders?"

"Yes," replied the king.

The crowd gasped again.

"The man is obviously lying to save his own life," said Trunculin. "As I've said, the firstman is in charge of the soldiers. If a few of his soldiers cannot be controlled, how is that my responsibility?"

"The king will decide that," said Stathen. "You may take him away now. Since we are beginning with your most recent crimes, who arranged the alliance with the father of Extatumm? It was the firstcouncilor. Not only did he have agents going to Extatumm in secret, but he has been working with them for many, many years."

Trunculin replied, "Yes, I did have the idea for the alliance. I wanted our new king to have a firm accomplishment. Forgive me, my king, if I was looking out for your legacy. There was no way to know that Extatumm wanted to destroy other kingdoms."

"It came as quite a surprise to the other kingdoms that they had such a large army of airships. These airships could not have been built in a short time. It took years to build such a fleet. Good people, councilors, you may ask yourself how this was accomplished. This was possible because years ago Trunculin sold the airship plans to them. He even supplied gas for their airships in the beginning."

"Next, our former king will be telling you that I am responsible for the rains falling on your head." There were laughs heard in the crowds. "My good people, I am simply a councilor working for the good of the kingdom. To suggest that I am powerful enough to do all of these ridiculous things should be impossible for any of you to believe."

"Yes. It is hard to believe," Stathen said. "That one man could amass so much power, and that one person could do all of these things secretly and without anyone seeing him do it, and then blame others for all of his crimes. I have proof, but first I want all of you to understand all the efforts the firstcouncilor has undertaken to cover over his crimes."

Trunculin added, "And don't forget to blame me when the kingdom shook about ten years ago, or that eclipse of the sun…"

"Perhaps not that. But I will blame you for the death of a king," said Stathen.

The crowd reacted again, as did many of the councilors. Asa tapped his staff for quiet.

"That is a lie. I never killed anyone," replied Trunculin.

"No. You never wielded the knife. Your ways are much more subtle, but it makes you no less guilty. Good people, imagine for a moment that you are the firstcouncilor for the most loved king of his time. Then imagine that the king and queen discovered some very bad things you had done. If you are an evil man, like the firstcouncilor, then you would have the king killed, forced the queen to flee, and then try to kill her later."

"Lies!" Yelled Trunculin.

"But that would not be enough," Stathen continued. "You would have to make the man the most hated king in history. How could you turn the most loved king into the most hated? Slavery. The most evil thing one man can do to another is enslave him. King Daymer was not a slaver king. He uncovered the slavery that the firstcouncilor had ordered. Trunculin got slaves from the father of Extatumm in exchange for the plans to the airship."

"These are all outrageous lies! If the crimes that you are speaking of were not so horrible, then I would laugh at them. This is the stuff of legends and myths. The king was murdered, yes, but my only crime was not telling the world who did it. The Firstman Brenddel killed the king."

King Asa used his staff to quiet the crowds.

Brenddel walked to the center of the stage. "People of the kingdom, I did kill King Daymer."

The audience was shocked.

"After this trial is over, I will stand trial for his murder. I believed Trunculin's lies, but there is no excuse for what I did. Trunculin sent me to inspect the gas fields knowing that I would find slaves there. He told me the king and the queen were responsible. It sounded convincing at the time. But again, I have no excuse. Then I found my own ... my own mother being worked as a slave. The lies that filled my head and my rage are why I killed the king. That is the reason. It does not excuse my crime." Brenddel turned to the queen and got on one knee. "My queen, I cannot ask your forgiveness for what I did. But I hope that you can understand why I thought I had no choice."

The firstcouncilor started clapping and addressed the crowd. "It is fitting that we are on a stage. Because what you're seeing are all performances. It's obvious what they're doing. I am old and no longer useful, and so for all my years of faithful service, they decide to make up lies to cast me as the most evil villain of all time."

"Your evil knows no constraint," said Stathen. "Did you know, good people, that King Asa and King Gordon were close friends? And they were chosen one right after the other. If I was a gambling man, and I am, I would say those odds are the most amazing I've ever heard. Why? Because the choosing of a king has been corrupted for a very long time." The former king motioned for two guards to approach. Each had a barrel. When they got to the center of the stage, Stathen knocked over both barrels, spilling name boards out over the stage.

The former king held the name board for each of the barrels. "Asa and Gordon. Hundreds of them. How? There are tunnels directly underneath the choosing tower. The night before the choosing, whatever name the firstcouncilor wishes is placed in the tower. The innocent boy or girl who picks the name can only choose whatever name the councilor wishes. I assume even my name was truly chosen by Trunculin. What Gordon, Asa, and I all have in common is that we are all poor boys from a small village. At thirteen years old, I thought it my duty to obey the firstcouncilor. Control the king and you control the kingdom."

Trunculin countered. "Lies upon lies upon lies. And still no proof of anything. Those wooden name boards could easily have been painted this morning. There's no proof that these were in the tower. All of these claims so far have been ridiculous."

"The proof will come soon, but there's one more thing I would like to show to the people. All of these things take a great deal of planning and a very long time to put these plans into motion. And there is something else that will shock you all." Stathen turned to the council members. "Good councilors, if there is anyone of you who has been on the council longer than Trunculin, please stand up."

All the councilors looked to each other, but no one stood up.

"That is because Trunculin has been the firstcouncilor for a lot longer than anyone realizes. Queen Ellice, if you could bring forth the proof and explain."

"Don't let this slaver scum speak, my king!" shouted Trunculin.

Asa slammed his staff down again. The king nodded, and Ellice took the stage.

The queen had a book in her hand. She came to the center and opened it. "After my husband was killed, and Trunculin tried to kill me, I decided to find out what the firstcouncilor was truly up to. What I found surprised even me. This is a diary from a king of Dard. It is old, and these pages date from over one hundred and thirty years ago. It reads, 'the young councilor Trunculin impressed me with his knowledge of history. He seems to be an ambitious young man. He is bound to be firstcouncilor one day.' When I found this, I assumed it was some-one else with the same name. Of course, it had to be, no man can live that long. But the old king liked to draw in his own diary. This is a sketch of the firstcouncilor."

She held it up for all to see. Trunculin tried to grab it casually, but she walked to King Asa and gave it to him.

The king said, "It is Trunculin."

The audience seemed numb from all the shocking accusations.

"Enough. Enough," shouted Trunculin. "Good people, you hear how insane these claims are. She sketches my likeness in an old book and now, I am some ancient monster come out of history to. What? Destroy a kingdom? I have done just the opposite. I have spent my entire life working for the betterment of all of your lives. I have counseled kings against terrible mistakes. Are your lives not better because of the strong leadership of our kingdom? Do you think it is greedy merchants that better your lives? No, I did that, and the other councilors as well. Now, I don't want praise for all that I have done. The most I want is a polite nod to the service that I have given for this kingdom. I don't think that kind of respect is too much to ask for. But to be accused of these insane acts is too much."

Loren got up from his chair and came to the center. "You wish us to respect you for the way that you have twisted our kingdom from what it was supposed to be? My sister Ellice has found documents dating back to our first years as a kingdom. They show how our kingdom is supposed to be run. It was not supposed to be run by rotating kings that were controlled by one man claiming to be a servant. You're thirst for total power has corrupted this kingdom."

"And you, healer. What..." Trunculin realized something. "Did ... did you say *sister*?" Trunculin looked from Loren to the queen and then to Gordon. "No. It can't ... do you mean..."

Gordon came to the center of the stage. He looked into Trunculin's eyes. "Yes, firstcouncilor. I am the son of the king you had murdered. I am the son of King Daymer and Queen Ellice."

Chapter 39

Final Proof

Gordon thought he could actually hear the connections being made in Trunculin's mind and the explosive revelations falling into place.

Mantuan came to the center. "I arranged for Gordon to be chosen king to show how easily it can be done. Good people, Trunculin has betrayed us all. No one man was supposed to decide your fate. Not a king, and not a councilor. Trunculin has been rewriting the laws and history of this kingdom for a long time. The laws of this kingdom are not supposed to occupy an entire room in the palace. The rules of the kingdom were supposed to occupy a book that can be held in your hand. These are the laws that our kingdom was founded on," Mantuan said as he held up an original law book.

Trunculin laughed. "You have no standing here, Mantuan. That law book is ridiculous! It was written hundreds of years ago. There is nothing in there to help us in our modern times. Let me tell you something about the first thirteen. Some of them were the filth of other kingdoms, washed ashore on our lands because no one wanted them. Only four of them were kings, and they named themselves as our rulers. They decided amongst themselves who would be kings. How is that fair to the people? They have no idea what we face in this modern world. They couldn't conceive of the problems we have, problems I've had to deal with. When our beloved thirteen were alive, the water was unfit to drink. There were only dirt roads, no modern cities. Is that what you want to go back to? Things are better because of the laws that I wrote! Of course there are more laws now. There are more people, and there are more problems! And only more laws are the way to fix it."

Mantuan replied, "The people deciding their own fate is the way to fix problems."

"The People? The people can't decide for themselves, because they are only thinking *about* themselves," said Trunculin. "I have had to think about the entire kingdom, and the greater good for all of us. Left to their own decision-making, what do they do? They gamble, drink, gossip, and spend all their time on distractions, never thinking of their neighbors. Every man and woman is a tiny part of the great machine that is this kingdom. But you would have them decide for themselves where they fit. The wheels and gears don't fit together on their own. I do that. Anything else is chaos!"

Mantuan spoke, "Good people, he makes a compelling argument. Should one man have total control of the kingdom? Or maybe a handful of men?" Indicating the councilors, "other kingdoms work that way. Why not have a small group of men decide how we should live our lives? Why have a councilor at all? We could just have one king decide everything, including what you eat, how you sleep, and what you can do in your own houses.

"But the first thirteen had a different idea ... an idea that is good and true, no matter how many centuries have gone by. The one thing the councilor forgets to talk about is freedom ... the freedom to do as you wish, as long as it does not hurt another person. Even the freedom to make mistakes. You look at these councilors and you think to yourselves that they know so much more than you do, that they are so much smarter than you. Are they? Perhaps they have read a few more books than you have. Have they gotten the right lessons out of those books? They have been convinced by the firstcouncilor that you cannot be in charge of your own lives. Have they been convinced that they are not men and women just like you? But somehow above you, better than you? These men believe they are entitled to control your lives.

Do they deserve to rule over you? That is not the kingdom the first thirteen built. Is that the kind of kingdom that you want to live in?"

"How dare you insult these councilors." said Trunculin. "They have served the kingdom with distinction. How dare you call their character into question."

Mantuan continued. "I do not question their character. I simply point out that they are men just like any other man. These men are no better and no worse than everyone out there. That is what I mean. And that has been forgotten." He turned to the councilors. "You do not rule these people. You are supposed to speak for them. Did you know, good people that all councilors were supposed to be chosen at random just like the king? Those men are supposed to be you. Does anyone here remember choosing councilors? No, they get 'chosen' by Trunculin because of who their family is, or their connections, or somebody they know. They no longer represent you. They no longer respect you."

"That law was changed because when we were constantly choosing councilors, the choosing's were endless," Trunculin explained. "So much time was spent on the choosing of councilors, that nothing got done. It was decided that men need to be chosen by their equals and that they should serve for a long time. Experience counts. If we were to choose from the people every few years, it would take them that long just to learn how things are done in the palace. No laws would ever be passed."

"And did the people decide to make this change? Or did you decide for them?"

"I decided on the people's behalf. I used my own judgment, but it was for the people. We *represent* the people. Do you want every little item to come before the people, or the mobs to raise their hands on every little issue? More chaos!"

"So you chose to take the decision away from the people? What assurances do the people have? They no longer get to decide any issues themselves, but they have to trust in your judgment that you will be the kind overlord of their wishes? That is not freedom."

Trunculin was about to answer when Stathen said, "I would like to call only two more people to this trial. The Firsthealer Corinn."

No, thought Trunculin. *No, please.*

Corinn walked out and stood, looking only at Stathen.

Trunculin has convinced himself that he only needed his mind to survive. He didn't need others. Corinn had changed that, if only for a brief time. She was the only person that knew even a sliver of the real him. *Now she betrays me too.*

Stathen said, "Firsthealer Corinn, do you have evidence that Trunculin is not what he appears to be?"

"Yes, I witnessed the Firstcouncilor's unnatural age. One morning, he told me to find a certain mystic. He was frail, what the mystic did …"

"Stop …" Trunculin's voice seemed tired. "Stop. This is her account of what someone else supposedly did. Is this mystic here as a witness to speak for himself? If not, she cannot give evidence." Trunculin looked at Corinn. She would not look back at him.

"Yes, there is one more witness. I call Valren of the Mystic Guild."

Trunculin was truly panicked. He had an answer for everything else, but he couldn't believe that they got the mystic to testify against him. Corinn glanced at Trunculin for the briefest moment before yielding her place to the last witness.

The mystic walked into the middle of the stage and stared directly at Trunculin. His eyes made even Trunculin uncomfortable, no matter how long he had worked with them. He would never get used to the stare of a mystic.

Stathen asked, "What services have you provided for the firstcouncilor?"

The mystic blinked once and continued to stare at Trunculin. He finally said, "I have done many things for the firstcouncilor over the years. I have implanted dreams into people's minds. I have changed the opinions of some councilors, on orders of the firstcouncilor. I always look into the minds of the new king and report their weaknesses to the firstcouncilor. The only time I have failed him was when I attempted to install a vision in King Gordon's mind. He had a vision dream of his own before I could."

"Why are you here today?" asked Stathen.

The mystic took his time answering but eventually said, "The boy's vision disturbed my entire guild. King Gordon's vision dream started with him falling. It ended with the world on fire, which my guild interpreted as all of the kingdoms at war with each other. If this was the firstcouncilor's hidden goal, my guild wants no part of it. I cannot see into the firstcouncilor's mind. Trunculin's true goals are hidden to us because we provide a special service."

"What is this special service?"

"An ancestor of mine recorded that a young man came to him wanting to prolong his life. That was nearly one hundred and forty years ago. It was Trunculin. I, myself, have been a part of this process, which is difficult, and takes constant maintenance to ensure the health of the firstcouncilor."

Stathen said, "It is my understanding that your Guild will no longer perform this maintenance for the firstcouncilor. Is that true?"

"That is true. My Guild will no longer help the firstcouncilor in any way, or any other official of the kingdom. We regret any bad deeds in which we have aided him. The last few days we have told Trunculin that we were performing this art. We have not. His natural aging process has already begun. He will die like any other man."

The mystic continued staring at Trunculin.

"Firstcouncilor, do you wish to question this man?" asked Stathen. "Or any other witnesses?"

The crowds were loud and restless. Only three taps from King Asa's staff quieted them. "Any other witnesses Firstcouncilor Trunculin?" asked the king.

The firstcouncilor shook his head slowly and the mystic began to walk off the stage. Stathen asked the mystic, "Valren, one more question. Can the process be reversed?"

Chapter 40

Endings

The mystic stopped. "It can be reversed, King Stathen," he said looking at Trunculin. "But the effect would be most ... disturbing."

Stathen spoke loudly to the people. "Good people of the kingdom, it was the attempt of the prosecutor today to reveal Trunculin's crimes in front of you, all so that the king could decide his fate. The most startling claim has been that Trunculin has lived an unnaturally long life, while secretly controlling this kingdom. Do you want to see proof that this is true?"

Trunculin was enraged and his patience finally broke. "Enough! Fools, all of you. Yes. I have done all of these things, and more. I admit these things to you for one reason, and that is to show how dedicated I am to this kingdom. The first thirteen and the bits of paper that they wrote, that was hundreds of years ago. I have done real things for our kingdom. Things you can see and touch. The law is a living thing and changes with the times. All of the things I did, you call evil, but they had to be done. When you are fighting for the way things should be done, the correct ways, sometimes you have to do unpleasant things. You have to make nasty choices for the good of us all. This freedom that these people talk about? I saw what unfettered freedom really was. It was drunkenness and violence and people going hungry. You want to live in a world with no rules, no laws? That road leads to darkness. I made decisions for your sake, for your own good!"

"And the alliance with Extatumm?" asked Stathen.

"Because they are the future. They don't pretend that they are choosing leaders. They lead with a strong will. They eliminated all of the old superstitions and nonsense. The father understood that one man had to lead so that he could make the best decisions for everyone. The ideas of Extatumm will eventually seep into all of the kingdoms. It is the only possible future."

Asa thumped his staff. "You are wrong. It is time for the people to decide for a change." King Asa rose from his chair and walked down the steps towards Trunculin. "Good people, it is time for you to make decisions for yourselves. Is the firstcouncilor right? Do you want to be ruled by men who think they know best?"

The crowd yelled an overwhelming no.

Asa continued, "What do you think should be done with Firstcouncilor Trunculin? Should the mystics undo what they have done?"

The crowd was nearly unanimous.

The cheering died down after a long while. Trunculin would be exposed in front of the people right there at the trial. There were four more mystics on the stage. No one seemed to notice when they arrived. They made a wide circle around Trunculin, closing their eyes.

"The dirty mob deciding my fate?" screamed Trunculin. "How dare you think that you can decide for me. *I am the kingdom!* I make the decisions. Without me, you will all descend into darkness!"

Trunculin stopped and looked like he had a headache. He stumbled a few steps, but remained standing. The mystics opened their eyes and walked off the stage. Nothing happened for a moment, and then Trunculin started to breathe heavily.

King Asa was still standing near the middle of the stage. He could see Trunculin aging in front of him. His hair began to go white and his face began to change. Asa looked away from Trunculin and back to the witnesses. He tapped his staff. "You are all judged innocent and you are free to go …"

Before anyone could act, Trunculin had taken a knife from under his robes and lunged for King Asa. His knife sunk deep into Asa's back.

The young king fell to the stage, his staff falling with him. Brenddel fired a wrist arrow and it punctured Trunculin's chest.

The firstcouncilor fell to his knees, laughing. He raised his bloody knife for all to see, showing his true face to the crowds for the first and last time. Trunculin was already too weak to stab at the king again. His knife fell from his hand as the aging process sped up. He couldn't even wrap his fingers around the arrow in his chest. The firstcouncilor's laugh turned into coughing.

Trunculin withered, fell to the ground, and died.

Everyone rushed to help Asa. Loren examined the wound and thought it didn't look deep. It failed to hit any major organs. But King Asa's breathing was not good, and his lips were starting to turn a dark blue color.

Everyone was around the king. Asa spoke to Gordon. "We finally get to see each other again … and it ends like this. I think … I think your name would have been chosen no matter what." Asa's breathing was getting weaker. His lips turned a darker blue, and he closed his eyes.

Loren went to Trunculin's knife and smelled it. He rushed back to the king and, without saying a word, put something in his mouth. The king's lips started to look more normal, and he opened his eyes. He spit out the ball of zoress bread. It was black, and it hit the stage.

Aline stared, watched it crumble, as if it was made of ashes. A tear formed, but she wiped it away before anyone saw it.

Loren tore some cloth from his own shirt and bound the wound. Asa blinked repeatedly and looked around, his eyes wide, not understanding what had just happened.

Gordon said, "Welcome back, my king. Now you know how it feels to be dead too."

Asa breathed heavily, his lips returning to normal. "I don't … I don't think I like it."

They were able to stand Asa up carefully, and when they did, the crowds roared their approval.

"Behold, your good King Asa," said Gordon and smiled.

King Asa whispered to Gordon. "We will have to figure this all out, King Gordon."

Gordon nodded, knowing all the roads ahead were uncertain. "Later."

Asa was taken to be healed. Loren told him he would probably have a scar for the rest of his life. They helped him off the stage and past the shell that used to be Trunculin.

Brenddel took the poisoned knife for his wall.

Gordon walked off the stage thinking of the mural on the wall of the underground fortress.

He looked at the crowds, and to his family leaving the stage. He felt like a new history was beginning.

END OF BOOK 2

And a new chapter of history was beginning
But not just for the two boy kings
The world was changed forever
But when great power dies
It leaves a large, dark hole
What takes its place?
There are rarely happy endings

~ Llawes the Younger

Dear reader,

We hope you enjoyed reading *The Trials of Boy Kings*. Please take a moment to leave a review, even if it's a short one. Your opinion is important to us.

Discover more books by M.J. Sewall at https://www.nextchapter.pub/authors/mj-sewall-fantasy-author-california

Want to know when one of our books is free or discounted? Join the newsletter at http://eepurl.com/bqqB3H

Best regards,
M.J. Sewall and the Next Chapter Team

Author Note

Thanks for coming on this journey.
I hope you continue Gordon and Asa's story.
There's lots more that can go terribly wrong.

M J Sewall,

August 2015

Thanks and Acknowledgements

To everyone that helped me with this story at every stage, thank you.

But especially:

Anthony Pico
Brian Hall
Hillary Frye
Irene Getchel
Janet Wallace
Jenna Elizabeth Johnson
Michele Casteel
Nellie Sewall
Preston Frye
Rose Torres
Ryne Torres
Sarah Harris
Terri Jones
The McAlister family (John, Susan, Aidan and Colin) - Thanks again!

Author Biography

M J Sewall is from sunbaked and wind-blown California. Surrounded by crazy people in the best possible way, he will never run out of wild and wooly material to write about. To sum up his character and talent in three words: Modest, brilliant, and more-than-slightly hairy. That's more than three words. Just making sure you were paying attention. He is considering a run for the emperorship of Japan as soon as there is a vacancy.

For more information please visit MJSewall.com

Index of Names and Terms

Adinn (Pronounced: AYE-DINN) – King before Stathen. Almost died on third trial, saved by Loren, he was later killed in a riding "accident."

Aline (UHH-LEEN) – Girl that helped Gordon.

Alonnia (UH-LONE-EE-A) – Former queen of Dard, Grandmother of the current queen of Thure.

Anthsia (ANTH-SEE-UH) – Mountain in Dralinn, dormant volcano.

Arm arrows – Small wrist mounted arrow gun, i.e. small crossbow.

Arrow guns – Similar to crossbows.

Artoth – Kingdom of the gods, rules by two kings.

Asa (ACE-UUH) – King after Gordon.

Asgonan (AZ-GO-NAN) – Island between Extatumm and Artoth, in dispute for centuries.

Aspora – Land of 1000 kings. Large, fractured land.

Banner of the kingdom of the thirteen – White rectangle banner with a red triangle in the middle, surrounded by thirteen longknives pointed outward from the triangle.

Borenn – First king, kingdom of the thirteen.

Brenddel – Firstman for the kingdom of the thirteen.

Bryn (BRINN) – married to Jeduum, ancient Thurian king.

Coltun – Assistant to Extatumm leader.

Corinn – The Firsthealer of the kingdom of the thirteen.

Dard – Kingdom that was overthrown and renamed Extatumm.

Darion – Thurian King Russel's younger brother.

Denogg of the family Xoss – wealthy merchant of Thure.

Dog teams – Small carriages on wheel pulled by dog team.

Dralinn (DRAY-LINN) – Port. Dangerous, a.k.a. Murderer's Bay.

Extatumm – Formerly Dard

Eyonna – Queen of Thure

Family Xoss (Pronounced ZOSS) – Wealthy merchants, Denogg and Santovan are brothers from this family.

Fire gun / rainmaker – weapon mounted on airships.

Fortistaf (FORT-ISS-STAFF) – Sandrell's tormenter in Extatumm.

Fortress – Place where a group of people live in the haunted forest of Aspora.

Gantroh (GANT-ROW) – Narrow mountain range south of the Artoth canal.

Gordon – A thirteen year old boy.

Haunted Forest – Forest of large trees in Aspora.

Jannfarr – Thurian king of old.

Jeduum – Fat king of Thure, married to beautiful queen Bryn.

Jhalgon Fish (JALL-GONE) – Giant flying fish, also known as Shadow Fins. Can reach up to 60 feet in length. Their flight capability is narrow, they rarely venture over land. The wing seem to get them to great vertical heights, but their weight appears to limit mobility.

Jorann the blood king - Grandfather of Alonnia.

King Daymer (DAY-MER) – a.k.a. Slaver king.

King's Dice – Dice game.

Kingdom of the thirteen or New kingdom – Gordon's kingdom.

Lantovas (LAN–TOE-VAH-SS) – Firstman of Thure.

Lawkeeper – 1) Workers that attend to the great law rooms. 2) Name of elusive councilor being hunted for knowledge.

Longknife / shortknife or Great Knife & Smallknife –Similar to long swords and short swords.

Loren (LORE-ENN) – Gordon's uncle.

Mantuan (MAN-TOO-UNN) – Firstman for king Daymer, Has a patch on his right eye.

Mural of the 100 kings – Painting in Thurian throne room, painted by Ninian.

Ninian (NIN-EE-ANN) – famous artist, painted mural of 100 kings in Thure.

Ninnith – Blue king of Thure.

Ollander Adair (ALL-ANN-DER) (UH-DARE) – Thinker/founder of Extatumm, died in prison.

Outlands – Many of the lands are unknown.

Pact with man – Faith of the blue king of Artoth.

Queen Ellice (ELL-EE-SS) – a.k.a. Slaver queen, grew up in village with Daymer.

Rainmaker - fire guns weapons on airships.

Rolem (ROLL-EM) – Trunculin's assistant at the palace.

Ruins of Tanlum – In the kingdom of Artoth.

Russel the Great – Thurian king of old. Ancestor to the current king Russel.

Russel the third – King of Thure

Salenn the peacemaker – Queen of old, kingdom of the thirteen.

Sandrell – Aline's mother.

Santovan – Denogg's brother.

Savil – Large, strong worker in Extatumm.

Skyler – Friend of Gordon & Asa.

Sour cake – Cakes that Loren makes Gordon for the sweetblood, helped lower blood sugar. Purple medicine cakes that contain insulin from pigs.

Stathen (STAY-TH-ENN) – king before Gordon, two terms/ten trials.

Steppen – Dard king that wrestled the seven serpents, central image on gates of Dard.

Swamp rot – tranquilizer on the dart that Aline uses in the healing rooms.

Talinna – 8 year old girl that picked king Stathen.

Tanlum – famous old ruins in the kingdom of Artoth.

Tethon, Son of Torr – orange king of Artoth.

Thorny root – poison.

Thure – Old kingdom, a.k.a. kingdom of paper.

Tobee – Guard of prisoners in Thure.

TrTorrin (TRUH-TORE-INN) – Called the father of Extatumm, was briefly imprisoned by queen of Dard.

Trunculin (TRUNK-YOU-LINN) – Firstcouncilor of the kingdom of the thirteen.

Valren (VAL-RENN) – Mystic who tries to implant vision in Gordon's mind.

Yajan – (YA-ZSAH-NN) Island lands.

Zoress Bread / Dough – Loren uses to extract poison.

Preview from Book 3 of the Chosen king Series

Seefer made his way into the cave. The vast army of creatures echoed their welcome. Deeper in the caves, his thoughts turned to his journey. He had a powerful master now, even if he was mad. People were being flung from the cliffs every day now. No one was even allowed to see him anymore, this god amongst them. What do I care, as long as I make my little toys, I am safe.

Seefer did not worry about anyone stopping him as he searched, he was protected now. The beatings and teasing he suffered as a child were distant, yet painful memories. My mind saved me, he thought as the cave drew darker, I can build things, and I know how to be important to powerful people. Besides, he had nothing of value, not to anyone else. He laughed to himself as he realized that even if he was robbed, no marauder would ever understood what he had in his hands. But he knew he would soon have another batch of one of the most valuable substances in the world.

The chirping sounds were getting louder. They mostly stopped during the day, but these were easy creatures to frighten. Easy to wake. He was always quiet, never waking the horde all at once. Seefer only wanted what was left behind after their night of hunting. Precious droppings, valuable waste.

He wondered why the man has shared the secret. No, he wasn't a man. That bothered Seefer a great deal. The secret that three ingredients could make such a powerful weapon was now his. But why? Seefer decided to let that constant question sink into the lower waters of his mind, churning as always. Focus on the task, focus on the gathering.

There was little light this deep into the caves, but he had grown accustomed to that in his many visits. He opened his sack and took out his scraping knife. Seefer knew that he was made for this kind of work. He didn't mind the smell or the way the droppings felt in his hands. All he could think about was what he was going to make it into, after it dried. He smiled at the thought of the beautiful destruction.

Above him, the horde of creatures hung upside down, their wings wrapped around their bodies, uneasy with dreams of last night's kill. As he gathered his ingredient, his mind wandered to the problem of gods and men. Was his need to create worth the growing madness of his new master? Worse, could he convince him and the Queen that he truly believed in the living god that she worshiped? The god was getting crueler by the day. Men thrown from the cliffs for even the smallest mistake, or slip of the tongue. But he would have to pretend to love the monster, and build more toys.

He collected all he would need for the next batch, and stood up with his sack, making his way to the light. It was a long journey back into the jungle. He smiled, thinking of the secret he had been shown. Now he had to focus on the task, calculating how fast he could make the dark powder. The god was demanding more and more. He kept just enough powder to protect himself, in case he was summoned to the tower and the cliffs. He wondered if the workmen even knew they were building a monument to death.

He stood at the mouth of the cave, finally back into full daylight. He let the wind whip at his face, knowing the heat gets worse at home, in the jungle. He looked out at his world. It would soon change forever. Seeing the distant mountains gave him a chill. The inner rings held monsters and men. He wondered how the distant rulers felt about this new god in the jungle. The old stories say they don't let anyone rise above them. How long before they came and struck down this new god?

Seefer shook off his fear, thinking of the future world where his toys might be used by vast armies. The thought disturbed him and excited him at the same time. He felt a vibration, like his very thoughts of the future shook the living world around him. Dark times are coming, and I will sit at the table. Like a dark omen, the fluttering chirping sound got louder, until the entire flying army exploded out of the cave, flying all around him. Something strange and unknowable had awoken them.

Seefer closed his eyes, not afraid of the tiny flying monsters. Thinking of the future world, a smile cracked across his face.

END PREVIEW OF BOOK 3

The Trials of Boy Kings
ISBN: 978-4-86747-489-1

Published by
Next Chapter
1-60-20 Minami-Otsuka
170-0005 Toshima-Ku, Tokyo
+818035793528
21th May 2021

Lightning Source UK Ltd.
Milton Keynes UK
UKHW012058030621
384904UK00001B/190